I0547466

SIMONE

By Angel Berry

SIMONE

In the year 1930, the community of Potluck, Louisiana is one of divided lines - not of black and white, but of the haves and the have-nots. Of the residents of Potluck was one Simone Tout, a young woman of twenty years born an only child to a father who started the town school and a mother, Berta, who was proudly employed as a cook in the mayor's kitchen.

Two men - one you love, one you hate.

Georges Andrieux, the handsome, well-educated son of the mayor, is a man that Simone despises - a man who is more than aggressive in his determination to make Simone his wife. Berta of course is thrilled, but against her mother's wishes the headstrong Simone has plans of her own in the form of Cotton Neal, a young man who Berta considers as nothing more than a common thug, jailbird, and bootlegger from the wrong side of the tracks.

"Ain't nothing but a bunch of wild ass negros up in them hills..."

But to Simone, Cotton is the air she breathes - her future husband and the love of her life.

While Simone and Cotton prepare to run away together, the owner of a local opium den is found floating face down in the river. When Cotton is blamed for the murder he disappears, and while law enforcement work vigilantly to apprehend him, Simone is left to endure Georges' bitter, violent form of jealousy. When he threatens to reveal Cotton's whereabouts, Simone finally falls into his trap as he uses blackmail as a form of revenge.

Toni...

You run away only to have your car break down on the side of the road. You accidentally murder the mother of a good samaritan...

The events that follow will change the lives of each woman forever.

Thank you Isa

PROLOGUE

"Now calm down, Delphine. Calm down!"

Deputy Gray stood in the bathroom and fought to separate the two brawling women. Once in between them, she attempted to coax the butcher knife from Delphine's hand though she swung it out in front of her with so much ferocity that the pink, terry cloth robe she wore gaped open to expose her naked body and the dark stretch marks that ran jagged lines across her breasts and down the still rounded flesh of her abdomen. Instead of her complexion carrying the warm afterglow of pregnancy, she appeared haggard and dull. The thin hair remaining on her head stood out around patches of bald.

"Get that bitch the fuck away from me!" She lunged again, screaming in such an uncontrollable rage that spittle flew from her mouth. Her eyes burned with the insanity of a madwoman.

"She just wants to take care of you, hon." Gray spoke softly and attempted to direct Delphine's attention toward herself, but behind the deputy's back, Stella mouthed violent threats to agitate her daughter.

After several more unsuccessful attempts to squirm past the deputy, Delphine grew exhausted and finally sagged into Gray's arms. She reluctantly relinquished the knife. Gray threw an arm over her shoulder and gently led her out of the bathroom and down the stairs then through the living room and out onto the porch. Once outside, Delphine sighed with relief – refreshed by the sudden fresh air that cooled her feverish skin. They passed the freshly painted red mailbox where *BAPTISTE* stood out in bold letters and Delphine relaxed while Gray neatly folded her into the front seat of a squad car.

Gray disappeared back onto the dark, enclosed porch and into the house. Moments later Stella appeared, still smiling but calm. Beside her, a young, sober-faced deputy led her down the walk and out into the cool, Louisiana night where she searched for Delphine with a relentless eye.

When she found her, she glared at her daughter with a

lovely, murderous gaze.

PART ONE

CHAPTER ONE

Potluck, Louisiana 1930

"Simone! Girl, would you hurry up!"

Berta Tout's stout frame nearly filled the small hallway that separated the kitchen from the sitting room. At the end of the hall sat an open bedroom door and she eyed it, impatiently tapped her foot and rested fleshy fists on her full hips and waited. When Simone finally emerged, Berta's plump, dark cheeks drew back into a broad grin.

The young woman who stepped out of the bedroom was beautiful – petite and doll-like with almond-shaped eyes framed by long, dark lashes. Her butterscotch complexion was smooth and radiant and not at all diminished by the sullen frown that creased her brow.

"Bonjour!" Berta shouted with a slight curtsy in spite of her broken leg.

Simone pouted in response to the fool's grin her mother wore and fidgeted with the starched collar of her dress – a black and white servant's frock and itchy woolen tights that Berta insisted she wear. The white bonnet she wore was pinned down too tight and several hair pins bit into her scalp.

With her face fixed in an expression void of enthusiasm, Simone waited while Berta fluffed the sleeves of her dress at the shoulders and bent to adjust her apron – fussing with the edges of the fabric and smoothing it against the pitch black dress.

"Look at the silly grin on your face." Simone smacked her lips. "You're sending me off to the devil's house and you know it."

Berta threw back her head and laughed - a rich, feminine roar that Simone could pick out of a crowd. "Aww, she ain't so bad."

"Oh, yes. She is." Simone folded her arms across her chest and moved past Berta and into the sitting room. "How does she see where she's walking with her nose pointed so high in the air?"

Berta settled into her armchair with a chuckle and

grunt.

"The other day when I went by to pick up your pay, she says to me, 'young woman, I will be standing here in this exact spot at precisely seven sharp on Monday morning'." Simone frowned. "I mean really? Is she really gonna be standing there waiting?"

"Yep." Berta nodded. "And in the exact spot where she told you, but don't you fret none. Just listen to what she says and you'll do fine."

"Mama, you sure you can't work on that busted leg?" Simone teased.

"Hush yourself up," Berta laughed. "You're just gonna have to fill in for me until I heal up. Maureen Adrieux ain't gone bother you none."

Simone busied herself at the mirror with her bonnet, swallowing nervously while she watched her mother's reflection.

As Berta sipped her coffee, she asked, "Is Georges home from school?"

Berta leaned across the table and grabbed the town chronicle. "Why, puddin'?"

"Just wondering."

"Georges Adrieux ain't gone bother you none neither."

Simone doubted that. "He's just so strange."

"Aww," Berta waved a dismissive hand. "He's got a crush on you. Always has."

Simone turned away from her mother and walked to the coat rack to retrieve her cloak. *Is he home or not, Ma?*

She especially missed her father at times like this – times when she needed someone who understood just how much she hated Georges. Her father would have stepped in to defend her for sure. Berta, on the other hand, thought the sun rose and fell on anything Adrieux. Even now she watched her with astonishment.

"I never could understand why you don't like that boy. He's loved you since you were children."

"Obsessive," Simone mumbled.

"He comes from a very fine family."

"Spoiled."

"He's intelligent, well-educated."

"Arrogant."

"I've never seen or heard of him bringing a girl home to meet –"

"Selfish."

Berta shook her head. "If nothing else, the young man is downright handsome."

"Pretty boy."

"He is not perfect," Berta brows rose and her eyes followed Simone until she disappeared into the kitchen to retrieve her lunch from the icebox, "but he is a good catch."

Simone re-entered the room with a grunt of disapproval.

Berta was quiet for several seconds. She sat in her armchair with folded arms and narrowed eyes. "Simone?"

"Yes, Mama?"

"You stop seeing that Cotton boy like I told you?"

Pause.

"Simone?"

"Yes?"

"Well, did you or didn't you?"

"Yes, Mama."

"Girl, turn your butt around here so I can look at you."

Simone's eyes cut to the ceiling, but before turning to face Berta, she tried to work sincerity into her posture and facial expression. She only succeeded in managing a tight smile. Cotton Neal was the one subject she avoided discussing with her mother because Berta constantly ran him down.

"Did you leave that boy alone or not?"

"Cotton ain't been a boy for a long time."

Simone regretted the statement before it left her mouth. It was as if the words had sprung from her lips almost against her will. What she'd wanted to say was that Berta might like Cotton if she'd give him half a chance, but she knew by the scowl on her mother's face that now was not the time to recommend him as an acquaintance.

Berta wagged a finger at her while her voice rose with indignation. "Girl, you gonna get yourself into a whole heap of trouble you keep on with that no-gooder. You hear me?"

Simone bit her lip and fixed her eyes on the wall above her mother's head.

"I'm surprised he ain't went and got himself locked up again," Berta continued, her tone spiteful. "His family ain't never been shit and the apple don't fall too far from the tree."

"Ma!"

Simone was shocked to hear her mother curse in the very same room where Pastor sat just the day before conversing and heaping his plate full of smoked turkey and rice.

"Well, it's true. Ain't nothing but a bunch of wild ass negros up in them hills – thieving asses." Berta smacked her lips. "They got all them ugly, dirty ass kids. Make good, hard working, religious black folk like me and your daddy look bad." Pride gave a lift to her chin and she wagged a finger at her. "Do you know how hard your daddy worked? Did you know that your daddy was the first black –"

" – schoolmaster in this town. I know, Mama." Simone nervously shifted her weight from one foot to the other. *Maybe if she brought Cotton by for dinner…* "I'm just saying that they're not all that bad," she sighed, knowing that her mother was too prejudiced to allow Cotton into her home. To make it over the threshold he would have to lay bloody on the porch, and once Berta patched him up she'd send him on his way without as much as a smile.

"And so you got a whole handful of experience, right?" Berta snapped. "You been over in them hills, girl?"

"No, Mama."

Berta again narrowed her eyes. "Then what you talking?"

"I went to school with a lot of those kids is all…" Her

voice trailed off under Berta's agitated glare.

"So you wanna argue me down about a bunch of lowlifes?" Berta queried.

Simone shook her head. "I'm not arguing." She would never be able to tell her mother that she was in love.

"If you don't know nothin' then you better bite your tongue." Berta smacked the arm of her chair in exasperation. "See, that's your problem, Simone - you hard-headed. Now I've been in this world a long time - look at me."

Simone stared directly at her mother whose expression had softened with concern. A frown from worry creased her brow.

"I've been around a long time and I'm telling you that dealing with this boy is gonna take you down the wrong path. He's trouble. Now I'm advising you to stay away from him."

The Gutter was that section of the city where people of sane heart steered clear after dark – different than the debauchery that went on at the juke joints deep in the woods of Woodford County and nothing like the hole in the wall speakeasy's of lower New Orleans where henchmen sat with their backs to the wall, the Gutter catered to individuals who wished to indulge a darker appetite.

In the doorways of dingy, brick buildings the watchful eyes of ominous shadows lay in wait beneath the keen gaze of a lone raven who sat perched on the crumbling brick of a vacant structure. The cold morning was not absent of a strong wind. The sky was a frigid, dark shade of blue shattered by the gray of an approaching morning which had an hour before missed the departing, stumbling figures of the heartless.

The streets were near vacant of life – only the insane, high pitched laughter of a woman echoed off the cobblestone streets giving away the location of a couple who leaned against a building passing a bottle of moonshine between them. She was small and pale with smooth skin and bright *blue eyes. Her rambunctious laughter was bold, outrageous even, and she gripped the fabric of the plaid dress she wore whilst twirling in a merry circle. The filthy, tattered material caught wind and billowed out around her legs.*

In contrast, her companion was tall and lanky with ebony skin and grim, solemn eyes. A cigarette dangled carelessly from the corner of his mouth. He passed the bottle to the woman then walked out to the street to stand in the approaching headlights of a car, and she followed to circle about him, skipping and whistling, at times letting out a girlish shrill of high-pitched laughter.

The headlights of the car darkened before it pulled over to the curb and in that moment the baleful eyes which peered from lightless doorways stooped to watch from the shadows, gleefully taking note as the chill in the air suddenly co-mingled with the heavy cloak of oncoming peril.

Destruction exited the vehicle in a set of two – the heavily dressed figures wore burlap sacks fashioned into crude masks. In their hands, they carried the black steel of certain death. At their approach, the female's laughter grew more obnoxious - sinister even, and the moment she reached beneath her skirts, those evil brows etched in concentrated anticipation. When her hands appeared, both carrying the heavy, cold metal of devastation those sinister eyes gleamed with satisfaction. Labored, excited breathing filled those shadowy doorways.

The locked door of the opium den was heavy wood instead of reinforced metal though it was of no matter since treachery owned a key – discarded half a cigarette to retrieve it, and when the door swung open, the merrily skipping woman disappeared inside with destruction at her heels. As the sky turned a malignant, bitter gray, explosions signaling death cut the air, drowning out the loud, strained panting of malicious voyeurs before silence again prevailed.

After several minutes destruction fled the building with the woman hot on its trail. Death carried a corpse slung over one shoulder. The woman hummed a jovial tune. Together the four of them climbed into the car and drove away.

Only then did they nod with silent gratitude. They backed into their dark hovels. The rapid heartbeats of those shadowy figures slowed while a light gray sky threatened early morning rain. A lone raven abandoned its perch to resting pigeon. The automobile disappeared from sight.

CHAPTER TWO

The sounds of morning accompanied Simone on her walk to the Adrieux plantation. The small town of Potluck sat right on the edge of Woodford County and had a population of nearly 600 people, most of whose family settled and established the town several decades before. The small community was home to one church, a school, and a general store - all of which sat at the very center of town.

Simone had lived in Potluck all of her twenty years.

She and Berta made their home in a wooden shack on the outskirts of town. Though old, the shack was well cared for and decorated by Berta's knack for gardening and love of anything with color. Vibrant wild flowers adorned their lawn and in back of the shack was a small garden of tomatoes, cucumbers, and turnip greens. The river flowed nearby and was a popular place to fish. Years ago before her father died, she would regularly accompany him on the family's dugout where they would sit on the water for hours talking and fishing while sipping tart lemonade and eating

Berta's roast beef sandwiches.

Just as Berta had boasted, it was true that Jeremiah Tout had been Potluck's first African-American schoolmaster. It was he who took the initiative and invested most of his own money to build a new school to replace the old, raggedy house where Potluck's children attended - twelve grades all come to gather and learn – taught by an old, Italian nun who thought it her duty to rid Potluck residents of illiteracy. She even encouraged the parents to attend lessons with their children.

Once the new school opened, the old nun retired and left the children's education in Jeremiah's capable hands, and he worked tirelessly to keep the school running and the children attending. It was Jeremiah who at times dipped into the family's savings to put shoes on the feet of poorer children and it was Jeremiah who visited the homes of those children who had been pulled out of school for harvest season, and it was Jeremiah who became champion of the community when he suffered insult and a black eye to convince the meanest fool in town – Delray Jones - to let his oldest boy Junior finish school.

Junior now not only taught the first three grades at Tout Academy, but he also ran the school in Jeremiah's stead.

When she was a student at the Academy, Simone received no special treatment because of her father's position, and in fact, was expected to excel over and above her classmates with Jeremiah demanding straight A's throughout her years of schooling. He lectured her constantly on her great fortune – that she was lucky enough to have an education unlike the poor children who lived near the pits – what Potluck residents called the "hills".

These poverty-stricken children walked miles to attend the Academy – most until their tenth birthday when they were at last pulled out to help support their family. Hill parents were stubborn as mules on Jeremiah's visits to sway their decision and in spite of his best efforts, no children from the hills ever attended the Academy past their twelfth year.

But even the hill folk mourned at Jeremiah's passing and Berta (though she would never admit it in certain circles) was touched when odd items appeared here and there on their porch even months after Jeremiah passed – squirrels skinned and dressed, chopped firewood, and even the random sack of potatoes. As for Simone, she had been touched that Jeremiah was so well respected outside of Potluck.

His death came as a shock to everyone – so sudden and so unexpected. One day he was a strong, healthy man; the next, he was dead in his bed with a hand clutched to his chest, eyes fixed on the ceiling, wide-mouthed – the shock-froze face of the dearly departed.

Berta was inconsolable. Simone feared she would lose both of her parents – one after the other – but Maureen Adrieux surprised the townsfolk of Potluck by showing up the day after Jeremiah's death and sitting a stiff vigil at Berta's bedside.

Simone remained thoughtful as she walked. The sky passed to a lighter hue of blue. She concentrated on the hard shuffling of her boots across the dusty gravel of the road and barely took notice of the harvested fields and the shadow of houses in the distance.

She gave old man Ulysses a nod when she passed him out for his usual early morning walk. He was a relic in the community – an ancient, squat man the color of black shoe polish with a head full of kinky, white hair.

The local children speculated that he was at least a hundred and fifty years old... or immortal – and had special powers that he wielded through the use of his old, crooked cane. Jeremiah explained to her long ago that Ulysses was born a slave, did not know his mother or his father – did not know his family. He had no children and had never married. The only time Simone ever heard Ulysses speak was on the rare occasion when Pastor could convince him to lead the church in prayer. He passed her with a hymn on the hum. She wished that she had the courage to ask him what he thought of the hill folk.

Berta came to mind and she cursed under her breath. She didn't wonder at why Berta and Maureen got along so well for so many years. They were more alike than Berta cared to admit – both self-righteous to the point of looking down their nose at less fortunate beings. Their gossip and the gossip of those like them kept the hill people as the lowest caste of the county – not in wealth but importance. They hated both the poor blacks and whites alike. They curled their noses at the habit of several people living all together in one raggedy cabin. They frowned at the hill children's wild hair and blunt speech. They chastened their own children not to look at them, not to touch them – threatened spanking if they dared play with them.

At the very upper class of Potluck sat the Adrieux family which consisted of the mayor, Raymond Adrieux, his standoffish wife, Maureen, and their only son, Georges. They were very prominent in the community with Raymond having sat on the town council for many years before being elected mayor, but after election, his visits to Potluck became infrequent and instead of socializing with the townspeople, he preferred instead to spend his time with other wealthy blacks from neighboring communities.

Raymond was a short, heavyset man – was known for his shiny, almond-colored bald head and easy wit. His suits were consistently tailored and he ever wore an antique gold watch that hung from a vest pocket – that and a diamond ring which adorned his fat pinkie finger. He quoted Frederick Douglass yet always had a ready excuse not to shake hands with a poor man, but he was loud and vocal in his staunch support and admiration for Marcus Garvey.

His wife, Maureen, was tall and unnaturally skinny, a plain mulatto woman whose disposition showed in her pinched face. She was strait-laced, thought herself regal, always wore black as if in mourning though she was adamant that her attire was only meant to express her deep devotion to her "religion". She was hyper by nature and always in a constant state of flux, which drove the servants crazy because she rarely left home except on Sunday mornings when she graced the town of Potluck with her presence at the old Baptist church where she insisted on claiming the first pew by right, deferring only to the pastor's wife when it came to choice of seating – and as far as she was concerned, rightly so since in her mind she single-handedly funded the church – paid for repairs, hosted church functions, and paid the pastor's monthly tab at the general store. And in return, she expected him to bless the food at her table every first Sunday of the month. A meal that Berta was ever in attendance.

Berta had worked on the Adrieux plantation for as long as Simone could remember. During the summers as a child, she would walk barefoot down the tree lined road that led to the plantation – past the fields and scattered cabins that housed field hands to where the leaves of walnut trees provided a thick blanket of shade and guided her way toward the old apple trees and over fallen pink blossoms that cushioned the way until she arrived at the small log huts that housed the servants. When she neared the smokehouse, the aroma of smoked meat would cause her stomach to growl. With a child's awe, she would watch while the stable hands led the horses out for exercise and she would cheer for the magnificent beasts – long to touch with her fingertips the beautiful brown and black of their shining coats. And then finally to the main house – a large, three story structure whose columns were painted a brilliant, pristine white.

There is where she would find her mother, the cook, going about one task or the other, and while waiting for Berta to complete her work day, Simone would gladly abandon her books for a doll before running out to play with the children of other servants.

Now years later, the trek to the Adrieux residence was just as she remembered it as a child only today Maureen stood on the porch clutching her bible in one hand while the fingers of her other hand clenched a white embroidered handkerchief. She waited in the same exact spot where she said she would be and Simone quickened her pace until she stood in front of her.

As always, the older woman wore her long brown hair in one thick, braided rope slung carelessly over her right shoulder. Her attire was customary – a heavy black dress with high collar. Without a word, she turned on her heel and started across the porch toward the kitchen.

"The house is in such a disarray," Maureen said over a shoulder. Simone's eyes were fixed on the high heel of Maureen's boots. "Berta cannot realize how this *issue* with her leg has totally inconvenienced my entire household. A woman her age falling off of a bike – and let's not mention her size. One would think that such a large woman would exercise better judgment."

They entered the kitchen through a freshly oiled screen door and Maureen led her to the center of the room where a long, scrubbed wooden table sat covered with apples, cherries, peaches and glass jars. Servants moved in and out of the kitchen at times ducking their heads and scurrying away when Maureen glanced in their direction. Others pointed at Simone and made silly faces while Maureen flitted around the table instructing Simone on her way of canning.

"Do you understand?" Maureen's tone was sudden and firm.

"Yes, ma'am. Ain't nothing I never done before."

"What kind of mouth hath you?" Maureen seemed taken aback. "We do not say 'ain't' in this house." She paused and squinted at her. "Nor do we ever, ever utter the obscenity 'nigra'. Do you understand?"

Simone lowered her eyes and nodded. She bit her lip because her cheeks burned.

Maureen startled her by turning abruptly to leave the kitchen. "And clean up after yourself. I would hate to have to tell Berta that you aren't working out. The last thing I need is a crippled woman in my kitchen."

~***~

"You don't want this ride, gal?"

Paul, the plantation gardener, stood at the foot of the porch waiting for her. The man was old, bent in the back and white-haired, an albino by birth. He never failed to drive Berta home after a long day on her feet. Even now, the old cart sat in the yard hitched to a horse. He nodded toward it.

"No thanks," Simone said. "I'll walk."

"Ya sho'?"

"Yes, sir."

He shrugged and turned to shuffle off toward the stables and Simone lifted the collar of her cloak before grabbing the porch banister and hopping to the ground. In the fields, men and women of various shades of brown worked their way toward sundown, and she waved at a woman who paused and stood to stretch her back.

The day had gone better than she expected. After canning, Maureen set her about doing the laundry – soaking sheets and table cloths in lye until her hands were sore, but she avoided being in the house with Maureen even though the woman popped in and out of the yard several times to chastise her throughout the day. Still Simone found that the work made the time pass quickly and all Maureen caught was her humming happily to herself.

As she walked, a breeze stirred her skirt and the hem fluttered gently at her ankles. When she made it to the road, she quickened her pace and again adjusted the collar of her cloak, lowering her head against the wind while fallen leaves and gravel swirled at her feet. To either side, the road was lined with trees – yellow birch and sweet-smelling magnolias whose branches parted as wind whistled through their branches.

She walked two miles before she heard the tell-tale sound of twigs being snapped by the heavy footfall of boots. When a dark figure leapt from the trees and easily lifted her off her feet she screamed. As she was carried into the brush, she beat at her abductor's back, kicking wildly with her feet while strong fingers massaged her backside.

As they disappeared deeper into the dense foliage, the melody of her laughter echoed off the trees.

~***~

When his warm breath fanned the supple, naked
flesh of her stomach shock waves of pleasure made her toes
curl. Beneath him, she stretched and wantonly arched her
back, moaning when the moist heat of his mouth enveloped
a taut nipple and firmly suckled.

When the velvety tip of her tongue found his lips she
eagerly explored his mouth – greedily until he moaned his
gratification. When his pleasure grew into a frenzy, she
wrapped her legs around his waist and reached between
them to caress the parts of him that weren't buried within
her and he groaned satisfaction while surrendering his body
to the dedicated manipulations of her hands and hips
moving sensuously beneath him...

She awoke to find Cotton softly snoring beside her.
When his arm tightened around her waist and pulled her
close, she cuddled against him and shivered at the warmth
of his body.

The back of the truck was cool. Moonlight shone into the truck through an opening in the raised flap of canvas, but in the shadows, the outline of crates tempted her – the lure of glass jars filled with Daisy's Moonshine.

Behind her, Cotton's chest steadily rose and fell. She turned over to face him and ran a hand over the stubble covering his face before pressing a kiss to his cheek. When his eyelids fluttered, she rested her forehead against his own and threw a possessive leg over his hip. Automatically and against her will, a worried sigh escaped her. If Berta had any idea where she was right now...she would have a fit. The mood now gone, Simone disentangled herself from Cotton's embrace and stood to dress.

She had no words to explain to her mother how much she loved Cotton. Berta would say that her head was in the clouds; that she would end up a bedraggled woman with several snot-nosed children hanging from her skirts and a lush for a husband.

But she knew better. She and Cotton had dreams.

Dreams that they were determined to realize together. It didn't matter to her where he came from or who his people were. All she knew was that they were soul mates.

As Cotton stirred, she chose a glass jar from one of the crates and deftly removed the top with a pocketknife borrowed from his pocket.

"Daisy's peach brandy," he mumbled behind her.

Simone sniffed the contents of the jar then took a large swallow before handing the jar to Cotton. She returned to lie down beside him and settled her head into the crook of his arm. In the shadows, she could barely see his face but she knew what his features held. By habit, she stroked the serious arch of his brow, the broadness of his nose, his full lips and the determined set of his jawline. With her fingertips, she traced the coarse hair of his chest and kneaded the hard muscles of his stomach. Together they stared up through a hole in the truck's covering at the glowing half arc of the moon.

"Prohibition gone get you locked up," she whispered.

Cotton turned his head and planted a warm kiss on her forehead. "No way. Soon I'll have enough for us to get outta here for good."

"Mm-hmm." Simone reached for the jar.

"You still wanna marry me?" he asked, suddenly unsure of himself.

Her heart beat wildly in her chest. "I really do."

He took a swallow from the jar. "But you still ain't told ole Berta, eh?"

"Trust me. She ain't ready." Simone laughed. "I'll write her a letter from the train station."

Cotton's warm mouth found the base of her throat. "How long can I keep you?" he whispered.

"Depends. You thinkin' on takin' me with you?"

"Only if you say it," he teased. "If you say it, I'll take you for a ride."

"No," Simone replied, pouting and squirming against him when he poked fingers into her sides.

"Please, honey."

He pulled her to him and bit the tip of her nose.

"Don't make me do it, Cotton," she giggled.

"Well, alright then," he said, shaking his head. "I guess this here is the end of the line."

"It ain't neither," she whispered, knowing that she would give in.

He smiled and she fingered the deep dimples in his cheeks. She closed her eyes while the rough pad of his thumb kneaded her brow. "Say it."

Simone sighed and sat up to settle on her backside. She took a deep breath and threw her head back then shouted as loud as she could. "Spank me, daddy! Spank me!"

Cotton laughed, guffawing and smacking his thighs.

"Now give'em," Simone demanded with an outstretched hand.

Still chuckling to himself, Cotton reached into a pail at the back of the truck and chucked a pair of raggedy coveralls at her. She quickly pulled them on over her dress before donning the men's cap that he threw at her.

"Be careful to tuck your hair in real good," he warned.

Once he dressed, he helped her into the front seat of the truck. After the engine grumbled to life, the truck gave a solid jerk before starting down the dark road. Simone pushed Berta out of her mind. She rolled the window down and let the cool air blow through her hair. She felt so free – the only time she ever felt free was when she was with Cotton.

When they pulled off the road and Cotton turned down an alley, Simone pulled her cap low and slid down in her seat just as they pulled up behind a one story brown building. When he exited the truck, she watched him through the side mirror while he stood at a door and knocked. She heard a muffled but gruff voice and strained to make out Cotton's reply, but the door opened and a tall, suited man stepped out into the alley. Together he and Cotton walked back to the truck and unloaded then carried several crates into the building.

As she waited for Cotton to return, she watched as three smartly dressed women approached the same door before being admitted inside. When the door swung open, music filtered into the alley accompanied by the remnants of male conversation...

"Look at the bubs on that broad."

"Nah. She's a cancelled stamp."

"No way, Bob. That there's a choice bit of calico..."

Several more minutes passed before Cotton exited the building. When he started the engine and pulled out of the alley, she turned to him. "A speakeasy?"

"Yep," he replied.

"What's it like inside? Hoppin'?"

He seemed unimpressed. "It's an okay joint."

"Well, I'll be!" Simone exclaimed excitedly. She had never been inside any joint – hoppin' or otherwise. There was one thing that Berta and Cotton agreed on. "They got the girls dancing in feathers?"

Cotton's eyebrows rose and his smile was secretive.

He struggled to find the right words. "Chorus line girls? Not really," he said, shaking his head.

"The men in there wearing them fancy long tail jackets?" she asked with glittering eyes. She was anxious to have a picture in her mind. "Bet they in there fox trotting," she said, snapping her fingers and swaying in her seat.

"Uh..."

"Well, what then?" Simone narrowed her eyes when Cotton scratched nervously at his brow.

"Oh, I see." Her lips smacked together. "A bunch of hotsy-totsies."

"I only got eyes for you, toots," he teased.

Simone scrutinized him with a critical eye. "You had betta."

CHAPTER THREE

A week passed with no word from Cotton, but every afternoon when she left the Adrieux plantation she refused a ride in Paul's cart in hopes that he would be just around the bend waiting for her. He was all she could think about and the temptation to venture up into the hills to see him was near overwhelming.

That was her thought process while she completed polishing the long, oak banister that circled the stairs. She was so deep in thought that she barely noticed Georges – backed right into him where he stood at the foot of the stairs watching her with the same strange expression on his face that he always had when he looked at her – stiff-backed with his arms at his sides, palms pressed flat to his thighs.

It had been at least a year since the last time that she'd seen him, but the sight of him still caused the hairs on the back of her neck to stand on end. She would have turned and fled the room but he was blocking her exit.

His starched white shirt and tailored slacks gave him

a polished appearance but his open gaze revealed his inner thoughts – the leering lust in his dark eyes was open and direct.

"I've been looking all over for you. Paul told me you were here for Berta." He was breathless, his tone soft and dainty.

The soft lilt of his voice reminded her of the very feminine boy that he once was; that he always preferred to play with the girls; that he avoided the male children. She recalled that he had been a stingy child – using his toys as manipulation to control the other children. The very first time she ever played with him, he pinched and pushed another servant's child – a toddler – off of a rocking horse because he wanted to watch Simone ride the painted, wooden toy. She had disliked him ever since.

"Just until she gets back on her feet." She steadied her breathing and tried to keep the edge from her tone. "Excuse me."

When she attempted to sidestep him, he reached out

and grabbed her elbow and an instant flashback of a run-in from their childhood made her cringe. He had always been too aggressive with her.

His eyes probed her – made her feel naked. "Simone."

She was transfixed by his mouth. Even as children, she could not help herself from watching his lips when he spoke. She realized then just how silent the house was. *Had Maureen went to the city? Where were the other servants?*

Fine, dark hairs surrounded his mouth. When he pulled her to him, she remembered the last time that they were alone...

The children huddled inside the barn and sought shelter from the rain. The storming and lightning had been ongoing for at least an hour and Berta had long ago shooed her from the kitchen with a spatula.

She sat cross-legged on a bale of hay and played with a doll. Willy, a teenaged field hand, gathered the children around him and entertained them with a tale about wolfmen while they waited out the rain. His voice lowered dramatically...

"It was not a dark and stormy night. Instead the evening was cool, the air crisp enough that leaves blew from tree branches, but not so much that Dudley couldn't keep his hat, and so his mood was not further agitated at the fluttering of his collar by the frigid breeze. A full moon showed bright yellow in the deep, dark blue of the starless night.

The steady *clop, clop* of the horse's hooves on hardened dirt was not as soothing to Dudley as it usually was, and he held the reins firmly in his gloved hands, but because of the pain in his lower back he sat stiffly in the saddle, grunting at times when he was jostled along on the unsteady terrain.

Dirty, rotten bums

Anyone who looked upon the man would think him a dour fellow. And they would be accurate. This silver-bearded man was indeed one of a dark disposition – a meticulously dressed man of sixty with wrinkles set deep in his forehead, thin, black lips ever turned downward in a scowl and beady eyes that hid beneath thick, white brows. He was a man of fortune and leisure, but to his discredit, he had an extremely impolite, rapacious nature about him, and therefore, was not considered a gentleman. And neither did he enjoy a good social position. But excellent social standing to Dudley, of course, was useless. Money, on the other hand, was of the utmost importance.

Now this man Dudley was a widower. His late wife, Biddy Jeffries, had been of a more avaricious and pungent nature than he was himself. They hated one another truly and he taunted her mercilessly about the broadness of her shoulders, the masculine curve of her jaw, and her dreadful mulatto skin which he found exactly "four yella shades too light". Biddy in turn – and much to his chagrin because she was right – would curse his "bald, black head" which she likened to an "ashy kneecap" and in that way the couple remained childless. They were married thirty years at least before it was whispered amongst the neighbors that old Biddy – who had swallowed her tongue but was rumored to have been intentionally poisoned by her husband – suddenly up and died. Dudley often joked that Biddy herself was the poison and that her tongue had finally turned against her.

A man of property, Dudley used his power as landlord to keep his tenants in a constant mental state of flux. He would raise rent on a whim, causing poor families to live on bread or evict an established business because of an imagined slight.

Just that morning, he had been accosted by a tenant because of a rat infestation. *And what was he supposed to do? How had the rodent problem become his problem?* And to top it all, the lazy bastard even threatened to withhold rent. *The nerve!* But after the terrible rumors that swirled about, one would not wonder that the unfortunate fellow might think Dudley soon desperate to keep what tenants he had. And maybe that fellow was right. At the moment Dudley raised his voice in threat, a lad sent to retrieve him to the constable's office solemnly informed him that yet another mangled victim had been found in another of his flats ripped to shreds just as the others had been – apparently by some unknown wild animal.

Well, to hell with the animal and the

dead tenant. Who was going to clean up the mess?

While Willy wove his tale, Simone took the opportunity to slip from the barn undetected. Her plan was to invade and explore the forbidden third floor. To her understanding, Georges was still off at the expensive boarding school that he attended in London. She would be the only child in the house.

Exploration would ease her boredom and Willy's story had put her in the mind to give herself a good scare. She would walk the long, dark hallways of the forgotten floor while holding a lone, flickering candle. There she would make too much of shadows that danced along the walls.

Intending to avoid Berta, she decided against sneaking through the kitchen and instead skirted around back of the house and took the damp, wooden steps to the abandoned floor. When her bare feet touched the landing, she wiggled her toes on the cold floor and removed the key from beneath a mat. Once inside, she lit Georges' secret candle and smiled as *light flickered and played over the walls. As she made her way down the hall, she used her hands to make the shadows dance. At times, she contorted her body into creatures resembling those from her lesson book on dinosaurs.*

Past empty bedrooms she walked playing with shadows until they doubled – playing in shadows until she heard breathing other than her own.

She knew it was him before she turned to face him – before he reached out to touch her because the hairs on the back of her neck stood on end. She was not prepared for the shove that sent her flying into an open bedroom.

Georges was a tall boy for his twelve years – chestnut brown with a wide nose, full lips and dark expressive eyes. His hair was fine and curly. A wayward lock fell over one thickly browed eye.

Simone, though tomboyish, was extremely petite for her nine years and flew through the air like light weight. She scurried across the floor to right the candle and glared at him when she was again on her feet.

As always, he was not shy in his observation of her and openly looked her over from head to toe – her wild, curly brown hair, freckled butterscotch complexion, small bare feet and wrinkled dress.

She backed away when he followed her into the room, and when she reached the wall and could go no further, he reached out and grabbed her by the arm and pulled her toward him.

As usual, she resisted. "Let go, let go!"

She squirmed until she freed herself. Her first instinct was to turn on her heel and run but she was angry.

"Why did you push me?" she demanded with a hand on her hip.

Instead of answering, he simply stared at her, stiff-backed, arms at his side, palms pressed flat against his thighs.

Awkward silence followed but she refused to let it go. "Don't you ever touch me again, Georges," she snapped. "Ever." Georges touching her made her feel like jumping out of her skin.

A chill ran down her spine and the instinct to run grew stronger. His dark eyes were intent on her, piercing, and she knew that he meant to touch her again. She didn't trust him and she was suddenly very aware of the fact that they were alone. As if he anticipated her next move, he stepped forward and blocked her path, startling her with the quickness of his movement. He came at her with an outstretched arm.

"Sorry," he said. "Really."

His smile was apologetic and when he offered his hand, she stared down at it for several moments, unsure if his gesture was sincere. When she finally reached out and placed her hand in his own, the moistness of his palm repulsed her and she started to pull her hand away, but instead of releasing her, he gave her arm a hard yank and pulled her toward him.

He was going to kiss her! She knew by the way his eyes burned desperate.

"Let go," she yelled. Panic made her voice high and shrill.

She could feel the heat of his breath on her face. Sure enough his lips pursed. When his eyes fell closed and he leaned toward her, she screamed, but he refused to let her go and for several moments they tussled until he was so close that she could feel the heaviness of his thighs pressed against her hips.

"Kiss me," he said, roughly grabbing her face between both his hands.

Tears clouded her vision at the exact moment when the candle fell to the ground. She kicked at his shins with useless bare soles as the flame went out. But when the room was submerged in darkness, her knee found an open path to his groin and landed its destination with such strength and precision that he grunted with pain – forced to release her from a firm grip but still managed to swing a fist that missed her face by mere inches.

As she fled the room, lightning lit her escape down the long hallway. She could hear him screaming behind her. His voice rose tight with pain.

"I'll tell Berta that I caught you up here stealing! You

had better not tell...Simone!"

And she never told but now standing before him ten years later, she felt the same as she had that night – sickened.

He had always behaved as if it never happened. "It's been over a year. Have you thought about what I asked you?"

Her eyes rested on his lips – on the ridiculous handlebar mustache that curled into his cheeks when he smiled. An involuntary shudder ran through her and she bowed her head and swallowed bile that steadily rose in her throat. She wanted to leave the room but was hesitant to pass him – knew that he would use her movement as an excuse to touch her. His pupils were black – dilated. His piercing eyes made her feel dirty – as if she were on display for his own private viewing pleasure and she hated him.

"I think about you all the time," he whispered. "Don't you think of me?" His eyes searched her face for emotion.

The urge to vomit started in her stomach – not because she found him revolting but because she could smell his breath. She couldn't keep the coldness from her tone. "I don't want to marry you, Georges."

The hint of pain in his eyes was quickly replaced by vexation and his hand tightened painfully around her arm. His breath was hot on her face and she was overwhelmed by the lingering smell of his breakfast and the strong odor of hair pomade and too much aftershave. His bottom lip reminded her of a thick, quivering worm and she could not stop herself from watching his mouth while it twitched then relaxed – an unconscious result of his intent concentration on her breasts.

He spoke through gritted teeth. "You had better –"

Simone released a tense breath when the scraping of furniture being moved overhead halted Georges' advance. He released her and gave a quick, cautious glance over his shoulder while backing away. Simone wondered where Maureen was. She wondered if anyone would hear her if she shouted.

"I have a lot of work to do, Georges." She hurriedly gathered the cleaning supplies into a wicker basket and started to move around him, but he again blocked her path.

Now overly agitated, she snapped at him. "Back off, Georges."

He paused mid-step and weighed his choices by again glancing over his shoulder. When he turned back to face her, a deep frown creased his forehead. "You're going to give me what I want one way or another." His gaze was fierce and filled with longing.

"Let me pass or I will scream."

"As you wish," he said suddenly and moved aside with a dramatic bow.

As she scurried from the room, she could feel his eyes burning holes through the seat of her dress.

~***~

While Georges Adrieux stood in his mother's parlor and wracked his brain for a way to dominate Simone's existence, two small boys, Milton and Josiah, were shocked to see a dead man float right past them as they pitched their fishing lines into the river.

The children stood still as stone and stared at the mangled form where it caught and bobbed near an embankment of rocks. While it lingered, Josiah stood frozen with shock, but Milton dropped his pole and ran to take a look at the corpse.

Once he had maneuvered over several large stones, he stared down at the man for several seconds before yelling over his shoulder to his brother, "It's a white man."

When Josiah found his voice it quaked with fear. "What wrong wit' 'im?"

Milton rolled his eyes. "He dead as a doorknob – that what wrong wit' 'im. Help me fetch 'im."

"Hell no. I ain't touchin' no dead white mens. Firs' thing happen is they blames it on us." He tucked his thumbs into the suspenders of his overalls and stared down at his bare feet.

"How they gone blame a dead man on two lil' boys? 'Sides that, look like fish been eatin' on 'im for a while now anyhow."

Milton stared back down at the dead man with morbid curiosity. He had never seen a real, live dead body before unless he counted the one time at Uncle Dale's funeral, but that couldn't really count since Dale died of a stroke. The body that he stared down at now floated on its stomach though the head twisted at such an awkward angle that Milton could see the torn, bloated flesh of the dead man's face.

"I reckon this here is Harley Roy," he said.

"Get out of town!"

"Yep." Milt stood and dusted his hands off on his jeans. "Well, I reckon we ain't strong 'nough to fish him out no how. Best we go get help."

"What if he float away?"

Milton looked with sympathy on the disfigured visage of Harley who now bobbed up and down in the water like a maimed buoy. "How you think he come to be here like this, Jo?"

The flophouse was a five story brick building that sat just outside the city. After he pulled the truck to the corner and parked, he sat for several minutes and watched the door. Loiterers set up shop near the building and in the walkway leading to the door – lost souls preoccupied with the nothingness of the day.

Long strides carried him to the building and up three flights of stairs where along the way he passed open one-room doorways where inside held lives that dimmed one space and caused brightness in others – a broad shouldered man having a shave but watching him through a looking glass; a smooth-skinned beauty pinning nylons to red garters that lined silken, ebony thighs; Duke Ellington's voice following him down the hallway from a room that held the delicious aroma of fried bacon.

Near the end of the hall, he approached the last door and inclined his ear toward it. The muffled gruff of male voices was there coupled with the sweet lilt of a woman singing. His knock was bold, a solid three raps with the balled edges of his knuckles. When the door swung open, Larry's buck-toothed visage leapt upon him, nearly lifting him off his feet and snatching him inside.

> "Three blind mice
> Three blind mice
> See how they run..."

When he was released, he collided with the ground at her feet. She did not look down at him but continued to sing and he could not help but look up into her mouth as it opened – the lips puckering and creasing as her tongue moved, the thin, red painted lips, the nicotine stained underbelly of her teeth, the soft, pale pink of the roof of her mouth.

From the bed, Earl peered down at him from his spot on the floor. His legs were too long for the bed causing his booted feet to dangle over the edge. Still he lay nonchalantly on his back with one arm folded behind his head. From his lips dangled a Marlboro – the cause of the thick haze of smoke that circled his head.

> "...they all ran after the farmer's wife
> Who cut off their tails with a carving knife
> Have you ever seen such a sight in your life..."

In the center of the room sat a round, wooden table whose surface was marred by cigarette burns from times past. At the table, Larry sat counting cash – separating cash into small heaps. Larry paid Earl no mind. Instead his concentration remained on his task – a slow lick of his thumb and index finger before the bills flicked smoothly through his hands while his lips moved soundlessly in count.

"Hell you doing here, boy?"

Cotton hated Earl – had always hated Earl. Not because he was a racist, but because he was the ugliest motherfucker that he had ever seen in his life. Entire life. And he made mention of this to Earl every chance he got. Even now when payday was moments away, his skin held the same pasty white pallor of death that Cotton had long ago assumed he was born with. Years of heavy smoking had yellowed and hardened the white skin around his mouth. Hard hill living and heavy drinking creased his face and prematurely grayed his hair – made his wrinkled forehead give him the appearance of a sullen bulldog. His eyes were too big for his head and dominated by too-black pupils – the whites almost non-existent and pink at the corners.

Cotton rose and dusted himself off. Larry continued counting. Earl swung his feet until they hit the floor and sat up in bed to glare at him. The butt of his smoke was now being slowly chewed in half.

"Hold him down, Darlin.'"

Cotton had expected it. He didn't fight – simply held his hands out at his sides while Darlin' searched his pockets and retrieved the revolver from his jacket pocket. Her hands made a slow exploration of his buttocks, lingered at his thighs then continued over his calves and back up again. She circled his body, her hands moving up his chest to rest at his shoulders. The smell of her perfume surrounded him.

He had always liked Darlin' cause Darlin' was just fine. Crazy as hell but alright with him just the same. Being crazy had its benefits. She would seduce anything, go anywhere, say anything, pull a trigger on anyone. And she would sing. Sing and dance while she wreaked havoc. Sometimes pretty; at other *times horrid. But always crazy. Yes, Darlin' was just fine.*

Today her pale blonde hair sat heaped atop her head in soft ringlets. Her peach complexion was flawless, naturally pretty. A pert, bow-shaped mouth now whistled while the insane, blue ice of her gaze lingered on his face. She grinned at him, stood on the tips of her toes to bite his chin in greeting before turning to Earl with a showy curtsy.

Larry grunted and propped a short pencil behind his ear. "$42,000 and some change."

Cotton squared his shoulders. "Well, let's settle up then so I can be on my way."

Earl lit another cigarette. "Give'em his cut," he said to Larry.

"Little dumpling. Little dumpling. Little brown dumpling." Darlin' skipped around him in a circle. The heels of her boots tapped loudly on the wood floor.

"There you go, boy." Earl gestured to a small stack of bills that Larry pushed to the edge of the table.

Larry took the pencil from behind his ear, roughly licked

the lead tip and made his mark on a small white card. "$38,000 and some change."

Cotton's scalp began to tingle.

"There you go, boy," Earl repeated.

Cotton ignored him. "Larry, you best be subtracting another six grand from your 'rithmetic." His blood began to boil. Did Earl really think that he would let him play him out of his cut?

He turned as Earl stood and stretched. Larry began to roll the bills with rubber bands. He stuffed the wads into a small bag. Darlin' moved to the door and leaned against it – one hand holding tightly to the knob while she swung one leg back and forth in front of her. Cotton could feel Earl's strange eyes watching him. Darlin' started to sing.

"What makes you think you deserve same share as me and Larry?"

"It was my idea."

Earl threw his head back and laughed. "Boy, don't act like you was some bad ass totin' a tommy gun in a violin case."

He was amused beyond his own comprehension. "I still don't

understand why you didn't knock him over yourself. You had a

key." He pointed toward the table. His smile was replaced by a

sneer.

"Oh, you gone give me my money – every cent," Cotton

said.

He pocketed the money on the table and moved toward

Larry, but Earl grabbed him by the collar of his jacket and

threw him back to the floor. Together they struggled until

Cotton straddled him, landing punches to his face with two

closed fists. Earl was the bigger man, heavier and stronger, but

Cotton was quicker, more agile and ducked the fat fists thrown

his way but took an unexpected hip to the groin that doubled

him over and left him sputtering on the floor grabbing his

crotch. Earl stood over him out of breath and red-faced and

Cotton glared at him – hated his hideous face, his ugly eyes.

When Darlin' began to scream, it shocked them both,

and Earl ducked – dove for the bed. Larry's mouth fell slack, a

crimson trail poured from his forehead to make a swift descent down his face. Darlin's teeth drew back in a snarl. Her eyes were crazed and animalistic. She swung the hammer with all her might. The sick sound of metal crushing bone filled the room. Blood sprayed the wall, covered Darlin's pretty face, dotted the whites of her teeth. Larry's eyes rolled back in his skull before he fell face first to the floor.

But Earl made it to his pistol in good time in spite of the sudden carnage dealt to his brother. The gunshot was loud and gave Darlin' pause – caught her mid-swing – and she, of course, carried the expression of one appalled and offended.

Like a cat, she leapt to her feet and quickly closed the distance between herself and Earl. Another bullet put a hole clear through the door, missing Darlin' completely, and she sprung upon him like a rabid hound. He tried to shake her, tried to punch her, elbow her – but her banshee like screaming startled him. Larry lying with his head bashed in frightened him. Darlin's fearlessness terrified him.

Cotton seized the moment and stumbled to his feet. By the time he made it to the table, the sickening crunch of bone *made him shudder but he didn't look back. Earl yelled agony*

while Darlin' pounded him with the hammer. The pistol

clattered to the ground. She continued to scream and ride him

– a wild, feral thing that he could not detach from his flesh.

Cotton grabbed the bag and instantly the light weight of

the wrapped bills gave him a feeling akin to exhilaration. He

backed away, never wanting to draw Darlin's attention –

wished for her to indulge her bloodlust. Earl screamed guttural

weak cries. He lay on his back with Darlin' atop him, the

hammer poised above her head.

In the hallway, Cotton avoided the open-mouthed stares

of those who peeked out of their rooms through cracked doors.

He took the stairs two at a time, making it to the second floor

before he heard the crazed tapping of high heel pursuit behind

him. Crazy ass broad. *He didn't have his revolver but he was*

not worried. She would never catch him. Not in a million years.

When his feet hit the pavement, he never took his eyes off the

truck parked at the corner.

"Help!" she screamed behind him. "Help! He robbed me!

He beat me and robbed me."

Cotton cursed. He was still several feet from the truck and he kicked himself for parking so far away from the building. People turned to watch him.

"Help!"

A slight turn of his head revealed Darlin' lying helplessly in the street pointing in his direction – her face twisted into a phony sob. Up ahead, two large, red-faced men stepped out of a storefront and moved toward him. Voices rose in anger and a small crowd started to form.

"Hey, boy!"

Cotton moved off the sidewalk and into the street. Just six more feet. Five. Four. Behind him, several people fell into a jog. A glance over his shoulder revealed that he would soon be surrounded. In front of him, four or five men quickly approached. Darlin' was the ringleader.

"He took my bag! Oh, somebody help me! He's got my bag!"

Again he cursed. There was no way out. With the key in

hand, he ran the remaining few feet to the truck but was too late – they were too close. He was surrounded.

"Hand over that bag, boy."

The first blow shocked him. Fierce fists and feet rained down on him and he panicked. The last thing he wanted was to be knocked off his feet. On the ground he would be stomped to death – or worse, overpowered and lynched. Even now he could hear Daisy screaming bloody murder.

He swung – tried to fight his way out of the enlarging crowd. Blood soon blinded him – ran into his eyes. He would not last if he didn't find a way to shake free of the gathering mob. There was nothing left to do but run. Though he could hardly see out of his slowly swelling eyes, the instinct to survive was his guide. Behind him the crowd pursued but eventually thinned after several blocks of heavy running. Even after he was in the clear, he still continued to run.

When he realized that he no longer had the bag, he collapsed against a building and sobbed out his frustration. If Darlin' found him, she would kill him. Inside his jacket pocket *sat the jippy cut that he had taken from the table. It was*

enough to make it out of Woodford. On his way to the train

station, he thought about Simone.

Gus Chester was awakened by commotion – the groaning of an engine, the screeching crunch of tires kicking up dirt, the mutt barking in the yard – but the noise of his wife outside shouting for him caused him to rise in a half-dazed panic, and he ran to the door hitching his britches as he went and stopped short when he came nearly face-to-face with Sheriff Marshal Bradford standing just short of the first step.

"Where yer boys, Gus?" Marshal turned his head to spit and a glob of tobacco juice hit the ground beside his boot.

Sheriff Bradford was bold and grizzled, wore dusty jeans and a tan button down that was darkened by sweat beneath the arms. A wide-brimmed hat covered a shock of blonde hair.

The confused faces of Gus' five children stared up at him. His wife, Margaret, stood with hunched shoulders and downcast eyes. As far as Larry and Earl, they were nowhere to be found.

"Why you askin' me, Marshal?" Gus was becoming weary of the routine. "Dem boys ain't no young'uns. They tends to they own affairs."

Marshal's eyes moved lazily over the weathered, frail man in front of him. Time had been hard on Gus. It was always that way for the hill people. But he was in no mood for games. "Harley Roy done been murdered and tell 'round town is yer boys was the last bodies what were seen wit' him."

Margaret gave a soft outcry but Gus' hard glare made her turn her back to them and retreat into the house.

"That don't mean my boys did somethin' to him." He was careful not to look Marshal in the eye. Instead he eyed the small brown pool at his feet.

"Well, I'm lookin' fer'em anyhow."

Gus dug his hands into his pockets and rocked on the balls of his feet. "Well, I ain't seen them none this week."

"Ya sho'?" Without asking, Marshal turned and began walking toward the back of the beaten shack.

Gus stepped off the porch to follow him. "Hey now -"

"Hey now nothin,'" Marshal growled while stopping to peer into a window. "I got me a dead man floating in the river and I want answers, damnit!" Marshal's face turned beet red. "Don't you bullshit me, Gus. Them dumbass sons of yours show up around here, you betta damn well haul ass to give me a holler. You understand?"

Gus shook his head and shifted his weight from one foot to the other. The faces of his children stared up at him in anticipation of a response. He exhaled a breath that felt thick with betrayal. "I hear you, Marshal."

CHAPTER FOUR

Midafternoon humidity brought on a heavy rain. In the Adrieux kitchen, Simone stood at an ironing board and daydreamed while staring out of the large paned windows of the kitchen. With absence of mind, she ran the hot iron over the smooth, silky fabric of a shirt that no doubt belonged to the mayor – a body that she had yet to see in the short time she'd been working on the plantation.

Had she been concentrating on her work instead of daydreaming about Cotton, she might have missed Maureen's irate form storming across the porch, back uncomfortably stiff, high forehead creased in a frown, fists balled at her sides.

"Simone!"

Just like that, her mid-day musing was cut short and by the time the screen door crashed against the wall, she stood at the ready. The same screen door had nearly gotten her fired days before when she'd made the mistake of propping it open for the sake of letting cool, fresh air into the hot kitchen but found out the hard way how Maureen felt about flies in her house.

"Simone!" Maureen shouted again even though they stood face-to-face.

Her creamy skin was flushed red, her smooth forehead dry under the plastic cap she wore tied beneath her chin. She slammed her bible down on the table and with a great show of agitation snatched the buttons of her slicker open and stood facing Simone with her hands on her hips.

"Why in the hell are those nigras standing outside my house?"

Maureen stood so close that she could see the fine hairs lining her upper lip. The woman breathed in hard, seething pants through nostrils that flared red-rimmed with rage and Simone flinched beneath the fury of her glare and took a step back with the feeling that Maureen was tempted to strike her.

She stuttered. "I'm sorry?"

Maureen shouted - by this time beside herself. "Do

you realize that I am the mayor's wife and a highly respected woman in this community?"

"Ma'am?" Simone drew back when the older woman took a menacing step forward. "I don't know what you mean."

"You're still messing with that raggedy nigra boy what live up in them hills, ain'tcha?" Maureen's mouth twisted scornfully and her eyes blazed, but instead of hitting her, she stood to the side and pointed to the door. "You carry your ass out there right now and get those heathens out of my yard."

Though Maureen demanded that she move, her feet felt glued to the floor and shame lowered her eyes. Why she felt ashamed, she did not know, but she was embarrassed all the same. When she finally mustered gumption, she made it halfway to the door before Maureen's shrill voice stopped her dead in her tracks. Her back stiffened at the words that were aimed purposefully for her heart.

"I can't *wait* to tell Berta this one."

She rushed across the kitchen with a nervous hand pressed to her stomach. Maureen's hot gaze seemed to burn the flesh of her back through the fabric of her dress, and she nearly ran from the kitchen, wincing when the screen door slammed loudly behind her. In haste, she ran across the porch and out to the front yard where a woman and two small, barefoot children stood waiting. She ducked her head when she approached and quickly grabbed the woman by the arm and steered her down the path leading away from the house and toward the apple trees out of eyesight of Maureen who she knew would be watching.

As they walked, she stooped to pick up one child that lagged behind and placed a kiss to the small boy's wet forehead before hugging him to her chest.

"What wrong wit ya?" the other woman asked, confused at Simone's uncustomary abruptness.

"You trying to get me killed, Helen?"

The small head beneath her chin moved, tickling her with coarse, sweet-smelling hair.

"Aw, don't worry none bout that old dragon. Reckon I wouldn't come all da way down here fer nuthin?"

They stopped and faced each other – one woman young and light brown, slender and comely and dressed neatly in a maid's uniform. The other dark and big-boned, wide-hipped and sassy, dressed in a worn calico dress and dusty leather boots. She clung steadily to the hand of a small, rambunctiously twisting child. A distressed frown lined her forehead.

Simone reached out and laid a hand on her shoulder. Her heart skipped a beat. "Something wrong with Cotton?"

Helen nodded – squinted in the rain. "Been gone a week. We was hopin' you seen him?"

Simone swallowed hard. "I haven't seen him for about that long." She shrugged. "It wouldn't be the first time he's disappeared. He always comes home."

Helen stared helplessly around the large yard while Simone nervously shifted the child from one hip to the other. "Maybe –"

"Simone!"

Simone and Helen turned to find an angry Maureen marching toward them. She stopped several feet away and peered at the children with an upturned nose.

"Now, Simone!" She was so enraged that her voice cracked. A pulsating vein protruded from the center of her forehead. She thrust an angry arm behind her and gestured toward the house.

"All that heifer missin' is a wart on her nose," Helen said spitefully while sizing Maureen up.

When she placed a hand on her hip and took a step forward, Simone quickly thrust the child into her arms before a heated word could roll off her tongue. She pressed a hurried kiss to the top of the boy's fuzzy head and backed away.

"Go on now. I'll be by later."

CHAPTER FIVE

Though she was miles from the plantation, her heart still beat wildly in her chest. She had borrowed Paul's cart...well...she told a stable boy that Paul *said* she could borrow the cart. If she failed to make it back to the plantation before he realized it was gone, she would be in severe trouble with her mother. But if she got back before Paul drove Maureen home from the fancy dinner Mayor Adrieux was hosting in the city, no one would be the wiser.

She held tight to the reins and took a deep breath to fight off a rush of dizziness that had seemed to come and go for the last few days and was relieved when a strong gust of rich, hill air hit her directly in the face.

Had it not been for the fear in Helen's eyes, she would not worry that Cotton was missing. It was not unusual for him to go days without being seen. She swallowed a lump in her throat. But there was something that Helen was keeping from her. She was sure of it.

The sun had begun to go down just beyond the

mountainous hills, crossing the horizon and turning the sky a deep red. Once she secured the horse, she crept through untended shrubbery and stumbled her way along the trail toward the shotgun shack where Cotton lived with his family. Nearby a lone dog howled, announcing the entrance of a new eve and the orange glow of a bonfire burned in the distance while muffled laughter met her ears.

She cried out when tiny, furry paws suddenly scurried across her feet scaring her into a jog. She was out of breath by the time Cotton's small shack came into view. From the chimney, white clouds of smoke drifted into the night sky and she was glad to see that a candle burned brightly in a front window. At the flimsy, wooden door she gave three steady raps.

"Hello," she called out. "Helen?"

When the door inched open, Helen's head appeared. "Shh," she said, holding a finger to her lips.

Simone was impatiently ushered inside and when the door closed behind her, a gust of air caused the candle's flame to flicker and illumine the frightened faces of the people within. The interior of the shack was warm although no fire burned in the stove and consisted of two large rooms that were clean but sparsely furnished. A threadbare rug covered most of the floor and in the corner a toddler sat bundled in a blanket and ate cornbread mush from a bowl with his fingers.

Cotton's mother sat at the table with her head in her hands and continually wiped tears from her face with a soaked tissue. Cotton's uncle, Ducky, paced the floor and took a long drink from a flask. He didn't acknowledge her presence aside from a slight cutting of his eye – the one that wasn't covered with the worn, black patch that hid the missing left one.

At the table near Mrs. Neal sat a young woman dressed in jeans and a men's work shirt. She wasn't that much older than Simone. Her eyes were red from crying and a dark bruise covered the left side of her jaw. Her blonde hair was plaited and wrapped loosely with a scarf. Simone did not wonder what a white woman was doing in the Neal home. Her presence had to have something to do with Cotton's disappearance. A sudden image of Cotton's beaten, limp body swinging from a tree pierced her heart causing her already sensitive stomach to twist into a violent knot.

"Any news about Cotton?" she asked Helen.

Mrs. Neal began to cry and Helen ran to comfort her. Desperate for an answer, Simone looked to Ducky for a response.

"We ain't seen him in at least a week now. Can't find him nowhere." Ducky again turned up the flask.

"And you're sure he didn't come home Monday night?"

Mrs. Neal shook her head. "Wasn't no meat to cook or no coal to burn in my stove. That boy ain't been here." Her hand trembled against her brow and she choked back a sob. "He done went and stole from the wrong people."

"Will someone tell me what is going on?" *Stole? Selling a little rot gut, yes, but stole?*

Mrs. Neal's face fell stress-slack. When she again

began to sob, Helen whispered comforting words to her.

In agitation, Simone whipped around to face the white woman. "Why are you here?"

To Simone, the woman's eyes seemed empty – void of emotion, blank. She stared Simone directly in the eye.

"My Larry is missing." She paused before quietly adding, "Cotton and Larry sometimes run together..." She shrugged.

"When them fools showed up lookin' for my boy, I knew something wasn't right." One of Mrs. Neal's palms slammed against the table. "I could feel it in my bones. If it weren't for Doreen, we wouldn't know nothing."

"Larry wasn't gone but a little while when them fellers come sniffin' 'round the house looking for him – scary type, you know." Doreen spoke in a hushed tone. "Seems the boys robbed some gangster and killed him."

"Murder?" Simone exclaimed. "Cotton?" A surprised hand fell to her chest. When she looked over at Helen, she wouldn't meet her eyes.

Mrs. Neal chuckled bitterly. "Girl, you sho' got them rose-colored glasses on tight. Cotton wasn't never no saint."

Simone disagreed. "He got in a little trouble but he was straightening it out." She turned to look at Ducky for support. "Besides, he promised me."

"And you believed him?" She leaned forward and stared at Simone with a rheumy gaze. "Girl, let me tell you something right now. I love my boy but he ain't got it in his blood to do right by the law – ever."

"With Larry gone, all I had out there at the house is the dog and a rifle. Couldn't make it to Old Gus on my own." Doreen interrupted. "Cain't stand my mother-in-law no how.

After the second time they come by, they stayed – parked right out in the yard and made they self real comfortable-like on my porch." She dug a tissue from the pocket of her jeans and blew into it. "Made me so nervous I couldn't even go 'bout my chores, you know. I locked myself in the house 'cause they'd walk around trying the doors and windows at all hours of day and night." A sob caught in her throat and she paused to blow her nose.

"The dog went and got his self kilt. Must've poisoned him or somethin'. After that, I known it was only a matter of time 'fore they tried to get in the house." She played with the fabric of her shirt. "Anyway, make a long story short, I shot me one 'fore I could get away." She wiped away tears with the back of her sleeve. The candlelight danced across her bruised cheek and gave it a purplish hue. "He had it coming too."

Simone leaned forward and laid a sympathetic hand on the woman's knee. She truly was sorry for her plight, but she needed to hear what she knew about Cotton. "Do you have any idea where Larry might be? Do you think he and Cotton are together?"

Doreen shook her head and sobbed into a tissue. "Probably dead, just like Harley."

"The body those boys found floating in the river?"

She wiped away tears. Her tone was filled with frustration. "After the robbery, I begged Larry to lay low.

Marshal Bradford was asking too many questions and the boys didn't cover their tracks worth a shit. Then Sheriff Bradford came around asking questions and Larry and Earl started shitting bricks.

Earl's the real reason for all this mess. Dumb ass told Larry that he saw Cotton talking real secret-like with Sheriff Bradford right before he showed up at the house asking questions about the robbery. Earl figured that Cotton meant to snitch them out and then make a play for their cut of the loot."

"Well, who has the money?" Helen asked, frowning.

"Cotton," Doreen whispered urgently. Her eyes were suddenly intent on Ducky. "After the robbery they hid the money but it ain't in the same spot no more. Onliest bodies knew where it was is the boys and Cotton."

"Maybe he ain't got it," Helen replied sassily.

Their eyes met and held for several seconds before Doreen replied. Her tone was cool. "Well, the boys ain't got it neither so what happened to it?" Her eyes cut back toward

Simone. "I was there when Cotton threatened to shoot Earl in the face for not handing over his cut. Cotton wanted his share right off the bat, but Earl wasn't having none of it. He wanted to wait until the heat died down. As usual, they beat on each other a little but then next thing I hear is Larry screamin' that the loot's gone." Her eyes lowered to her lap. "I'll tell you one thing, it wasn't just Harley's money that got took and them boys what lookin' for him and my Larry are meaner than any I ever seen. On top of that, there's a rumor going 'round that Cotton was the trigger man – that it was his idea to kill Harley and rob him."

Mrs. Neal began to cry.

"It was Earl got my Larry into this mess – that jackass with his bullshit schemes. I knowed what they was planning from day one 'cause I heard them talkin' 'bout it. Never thought Larry would go through with it though." Her lips pursed in agitation. "All I know is one day the two of them are standing outside tipping the hooch and shooting the shit – nothing unusual." She leaned forward and whispered conspiratorially. "But I was in the kitchen cleaning and I hears what they was a-yapping, see?

Earl's going on about some place where Cotton delivers whiskey – some low down joint they planned on robbing. Well, that was the end of it." Doreen rubbed her hands together to signal finality.

"Or at least I thought so until the sheriff showed up on my doorstep looking for Larry. Then a few days later, I wakes up in the middle of the night 'cause Larry and Earl is arguing in the kitchen. Earl is whoopin' and hollerin' to high hell that word in the city is Cotton done blamed them for Harley's murder and it's all over town. So now not only is the cash missing but Cotton is missing too." She stared directly at Helen. "You catch my drift?"

Seconds passed with them scowling at one another before Doreen continued. "Well, Larry got all fired up and he and Earl tore out the house to go find Cotton. Next thing I know, Larry's missing and whoever Harley owed cash," she tensed, "are at my door looking for the robbery money." She

83

reached for Ducky's cigarette with a shaky hand.

Helen's tone was soft but accusatory. "And you think we know something, right? Like where Cotton hid the money?"

Doreen averted her gaze. Her voice was barely audible. "Yeah, I do."

~***~

It was after ten when she finally reached the city. After leaving the hills, she decided to look for Cotton on her own since she was sure that by now only trouble awaited her at home. The dirt road soon turned to stone and the horse's hooves beat rhythmically on the red brick over the squealing of the cart's wheels.

Though she hardly ever ventured too far away from home, Simone knew exactly where she was going and steered the horse toward the center of the city. Patrolman walked their beat beneath street lights that illuminated the dark corners they passed. After several blocks, Simone stopped the horse in front of a small, brick building. As she neared the door, she pulled the hood of her cloak over her head. She knocked and waited a full minute before a metal plate slid back to reveal a pair of round, dark eyes – the whites engraved with purple veins.

"Yea?" a deep baritone queried.

"I need to see Daisy," she said and before he could protest she added, "It's about Cotton."

The metal plate slid back and moments later the door swung open to allow her entry. The doorman, a large, bald ebony man, stepped back to let her pass then closed the door.

Though the hall was empty it was clouded with smoke. Jazz played from the radio and five pool tables sat in the middle of the floor, the felt tops glowing bright green from the overhead ceiling lamps. Behind the bar drying glasses was a short, chubby woman with a bald head. A cigarette dangled from her lips and she eyed Simone with an expectant gaze.

"Took you long enough," she mumbled before

stubbing her cigarette out in a glass ashtray that sat atop the bar. With a tilt of her head, she gestured behind her and Simone looked to the far end of the bar to find Georges staring at her. His presence so caught her off guard that she fell into a bar stool. He grinned and awkwardly waved before running a hand through his hair.

Simone cut her eyes at him and turned her attention back to Daisy. "You seen Cotton?"

The other woman pulled a deck of cards from beneath the bar and began to shuffle them. "How that boy mama?"

"Not good. She's wondering if he done got himself killed." Simone blinked back tears. Over Daisy's shoulder she could see Georges staring blankly into his glass. She lowered her voice. "Do you know where he is?"

Daisy reshuffled the cards. She carefully laid a Jack-of-Spades on the bar top. "That den they knocked over was a filthy place, but it generated a lot of money." Daisy's voice was edged with annoyance. "Cotton fucked up."

Simone heart fell at the finality of her words. "Is he dead?" she whispered.

Daisy shook her head. "Not yet."

"Where is he?"

"Close by." Her tone was aloof – suspicious even. "He has to come up with that money or..." Daisy ran a fat finger across her throat, "...the hangman."

Georges cleared his throat and they both turned to look over at him. He continued to stare into his glass.

Simone ignored him. "I know you know where he is, Daisy."

Daisy flipped another spade face down on the bar. "Too risky." She stared quizzically at her next card. "Right now the vultures are circling. But don't you worry. I know exactly where to find him."

~***~

She exited the bar the same as she had entered, with a heavy spirit and slumped shoulders. She was relieved to know that at the very least Cotton was alive though Daisy had refused to tell her where he was – had refused to even pass on a message.

"Simone."

Interrupted from her thoughts, Simone turned with a start then sighed with disappointment. Georges stared down at her – already nearly at her back.

"What is it?" She was annoyed at his presence. *What had he been doing at Daisy's anyway? How had he gotten so close without her hearing him behind her?*

"Listen," he started with his hands out, "why don't we ride back together. I'll have Paul come for the cart and you can ride in the automobile with me."

"That's okay, Georges." The last thing she wanted was to be cooped up in a car with him. "I'll be fine."

He frowned. "I doubt that. My mother is not at all happy with you right now. It's best I take you home. I'll try and talk to her – you know, iron everything out."

"Georges –"

"I insist."

He turned and walked away clearly expecting her to follow him, which she did, and reluctantly climbed into the seat beside him. As the engine started, he began to whistle and she cut her eyes in his direction. The tune was jaunty but coming from his lips, it made her nose turn.

They rode in silence for the first mile and after the second, Simone began to relax. Again her thoughts went to Cotton. *If only she knew where he was, she would go to be with him.* She would have to make plans without her mother being the wiser. *Maybe she could hide a suitcase behind the house near –*

"Is everything okay with you, Simone?"

Against her will, an agitated frown creased her brow. "Why do you ask?"

"I couldn't help but overhear your conversation with Daisy."

Simone turned to glare at him, her mouth wide with shock. "You eavesdropped?" Her heart stopped cold. "That was a private conversation."

Georges' smile was eerily calm. "The place was empty; Daisy's voice carried."

Agitation crossed her arms over her chest. *Now what?* She didn't hesitate. "We're getting married."

"Yea, I know." His tone was barely above a whisper. "I can't believe you chose him over me."

His smile caught her off guard – made it hard for her to tell what he was thinking. His slim fingers curled tightly about the steering wheel and a lock of curly, black hair fell across his brow. He brushed it away with the tip of a manicured finger.

A chill ran up her spine.

"What a shame about Harley Roy."

He was trying to bait her.

"I saw him," he said, turning to look in her face. "Cotton I mean."

You're a liar. She rolled her eyes. "Where?"

"There at Daisy's. I saw him go in back as I was pulling in."

"I don't believe you." Her tone carried the edge of loathing. She turned in her seat and ignored him.

A mile passed before he again spoke. "What would really be a shame is if word got out that old fat Daisy knows where he is – that she's hiding him." Cotton's eyes were on the road, but the car slowed to a crawl. When he turned to her, his voice was hard. "One more nigger swinging from a tree."

She knew what was coming next and she shook her head and bit back tears. She believed him that he would tell. On that she did not doubt him at all. *Oh, Cotton.* She knew what was coming next and she cringed when his hand crept across the seat and came to rest on her thigh.

Oh no. Cotton...

Georges groaned and excitedly snatched at her dress. His fingers crept beneath her skirt to squeeze her thigh. She cursed him and swatted his hand away.

"That's okay," he said, his hand again moving to the steering wheel. The car accelerated. "Tomorrow I think I'll call on the sheriff. See how he feels about it."

Her heart fell. "Georges, please," she begged. "Please don't tell."

When his hand fell to his groin, her eyes closed with dread. "Touch me," he said, his voice breathless.

She opened her eyes to find him staring at her – lips parted in concentration, eyes glazed over with lust.

"Georges –"

He reached out and snatched her hand and brought it to his crotch. He began jerking in his seat then, interlaced her fingers with his own, cupped her hand over the hardening bulge in his pants. While they played tug of war with her arm, she prayed that he wouldn't pull over to the side of the road.

She fought with both arms though he pulled her to him. Still driving, he held her tight to his side, his shoulder digging into her chin while he held firmly to her wrist. He thrust into her hand, moaning and bucking his hips until Simone yelled with disgust. A shudder overtook him –

weakened him enough that she escaped his grasp.

"Georges!"

He sat back in his seat panting softly. A sheen from sweat covered his forehead. A satisfied smirk covered his face.

"Just remember what I said, Simone. I'll be quiet." His tongue was still thick with arousal. "But you're going to have to give me something."

CHAPTER SIX

Berta leaned against the table and balanced herself on one leg to watch Simone creep into the house. Fuming to the point that her scalp itched, she slowly lowered her body into a chair.

Simone hung her cloak up then smoothed her dress with damp palms. She could feel Berta's eyes burning holes into the back of her head. She took a deep breath before turning to confront her mother.

"Are you a damn fool?" Berta yelled just as she fixed her mouth to apologize.

"Mama –"

"Mama my ass!" Berta shouted. She was so upset that she could hardly form words. "Your daddy is turning over in his grave right now."

Simone begged. "Please listen."

"I asked you to do one thing for me. One thing!" Berta pointed a trembling finger at her. "I should've married you off to that Donovan boy when I had the chance. But no!

And why? Because you wanna keep up with that dusty dog in the woods. Now look at you!" Berta stumped her good foot in frustration. "How dare you leave the impression with Maureen that you don't have any home training? Do you know how embarrassing that is for me?"

"I'm so sorry, Mama," Simone pleaded. She hated to see the pained expression on her mother's face.

"You stole Paul's horse?"

"I borrowed it."

"Where did you go?" Berta leaned forward in her seat and looked Simone over as if she were a peculiar insect. "I betcha it had something to do with those ragamuffins come looking for you at Maureen's." When Simone didn't respond, Berta sat back in her seat and glared at her. "You lied to me. You told me that you let that Cotton alone – looked me dead-eyed square in the face and lied."

"Mama –"

"Maureen talked to that girl and she knows that you're making time with that boy. You think she's gonna keep that secret – that Berta Tout's unmarried daughter is gallavantin' with a heathen?"

Simone took a deep breath and tried strange words on her tongue. "I'm a grown woman."

"Then get your grown ass out this house!" Berta exclaimed. "That's what grown women do." She shook her head. "I can't believe you shamed me like that. And for some negro that ain't got a pot or a window." After several moments of glaring at her, Berta shook her head with disgust. "I can't hardly stand to look at you."

Simone took a deep breath and bit her tongue. Heat from anger burned at the nape of her neck and she turned and left the room before she said something to her mother that she would regret.

"Maureen don't want you at the house no more," Berta continued, her voice spiteful. "She's convinced that you gonna fill her yard with them snot-nosed crumb snatchers, so I guess I'll just have to work on this busted leg to feed us both."

A retort nearly sprang from her lips as she turned, but to see Berta sitting at the table looking dejected and ashamed made her again bite her tongue. "I am sorry, Mama."

"Yes, that you are."

Berta gave Simone her back.

~***~

Hours later, Simone lay in bed staring up at the ceiling. She was fully clothed beneath her blanket and entertaining the urge to leave the house and make her way to Daisy's to warn her of Georges. Had it not been for the fact that she could think of no way to make it the several miles into the city except by foot, she would have left the house as soon as her mother fell asleep. Even now, she could hear Berta snoring from her bedroom.

She did not doubt that Georges would turn Cotton in if for nothing else than to hurt her. He was a vindictive man and now that he had found a way to have her for himself, Cotton only existed in his mind as an object – a bargaining chip. *Something to torture her with. Something to use to bend her to his will.*

But now that Maureen no longer wanted her around, she had a better chance of stalling his advances. Of course by now, he had to know that Maureen no longer wanted her on the plantation. She fully believed that he would hurt Cotton if she didn't give him his way, but she was also confident that he would allow her the chance to comply. Knowing Georges, his plan would be to catch her in a room alone – somewhere in the house performing a chore when neither his mother nor any of the servants would be around. There he would threaten Cotton to intimidate and lure her to the third floor – always the third floor. But if nothing else, he was persistent, and she wondered what he would do now that she wasn't so accessible.

Like his father, he rarely if ever attended church on Sundays and would be an unusual sight at services, but she doubted he would harass her there beneath the prying eyes of his mother. Even visiting her at home would raise too many eyebrows and she could think of no viable excuse that he could use for trying to carry her away. Besides, the last thing that Maureen would tolerate was a scandal surrounding the Adrieux name.

Simone sighed, turned over onto her back and roughly yanked the blanket over her head. She truly was sorry for causing a problem for her mother, but she couldn't seem to keep her mind off of Cotton for more than a few minutes at a time.

She prayed that he would find his way back to her.

~***~

The following morning just before the sun rose, Simone stood at the window in her nightgown and watched her mother make slow progress out to Paul's old cart by use of a cane. With a caring smile, he helped her up into the seat and then slowly climbed on himself. He gave Berta's knee a reassuring pat before snapping the reins and leading the horse away.

The old woman was large – not fat but solid. She was strong. It took four heavy swings of the hammer to fell her. The first swing caused her to turn in her seat and frown at her murderer. When the second swing stalked her, she caught the hammer but it was wrenched from her grasp. She swung a desperate fist and relief filled her eyes when she connected solidly with the hard jawbone of her attacker, but the next swing of the hammer caught her square in the face – struck the bridge of her nose and caused blood to eject from her nostrils. The final swing brought her to her knees.

Once the doors were closed and fresh midnight air again filled flared nostrils, Daisy was left behind to burn.

"Get in the car."

Simone wiped tears from her eyes but quickened her pace. *How had Georges known that she would go into the city?*

He was the last person she wanted to see. Especially right now when all she could think about was Cotton.

"Not right now, Georges. Please."

The car inched alongside her and Georges watched her – his eyes excitedly predatory. "We had a deal," he said.

"I just need some time, okay?"

The car came to a halt beside her and Georges leaned over and pushed out the passenger door. "How stupid do you think I am?"

She refused to look at him and instead stared down at her feet.

"Get in the car, Simone."

Indecision settled over her and she cursed beneath her breath. Tears burned her eyes. *Had he stumbled upon her by accident?*

Georges yawned. "You know, I was gonna head home, but I think I'll go on down to the sheriff's office and see if I can direct Marshal Bradford to where Daisy is holding Cotton Neal."

Panic made her dizzy. "Please, Georges. I –"

Simone watched – panicked when he retreated. The car lurched forward and turned in the middle of the road to head toward the city.

Her heart began to pound painfully in her chest. *If Cotton was found, he would be killed.*

"Wait!" she screamed, chasing the car.

At first, she thought that he would keep going and in a panic she chased the car until she ran out of breath – until she collapsed in the road in a fit of hysterics. When the car stopped, she ran to catch up with it.

"Say please," he said, his smile mocking.

Tears stung her eyes. "Please, Georges," she pled. *Cotton...*

"Do it now or we don't have a deal," he said, his voice

hard.

Simone's head jerked in a nod of defeat.

His tone was as cold as his gaze. "Get your ass in this car."

~***~

Desperation forced her feet to move one in front of the other. She kept her head down and sprinted across the lawn ahead of him and then around to the back of the house. The last thing she wanted was to be caught. Georges seemed as if he could care less. As he rounded the corner behind her, she blinked back tears and told herself that she wasn't betraying Cotton – that she was simply doing what she had to do to keep him safe. It would not be the same as when she made love with Cotton. This was something different.

That was love. This would be different.

In a daze, she followed him up the back stairs – cringing because he constantly turned to stare behind him. The lust in his eyes nearly made her knees buckle with revulsion.

When they reached the door, he ushered her inside where she leaned against the wall for support – took deep breaths to ease an onslaught of dizziness – but Georges surprised her by grabbing the collar of her cloak and yanking her down the cold hallway toward his bedroom. Once they were inside, he slammed the door closed and turned to face her.

"Take your clothes off," he barked.

"Georges –"

"Now, Simone."

Simone turned her back to him and removed her dress, her brassiere, and finally her pantaloons. Behind her, Georges' breathing became harsh. When he approached, Simone tried self-consciously to cover her breasts with her arms. When she felt the hotness of his breath at the nape of her neck, she swallowed bile.

"Turn around," he said.

Simone turned, averting her gaze, cheeks burning, not wanting to look at him. When one cold fingertip reached out to touch her nipple she jumped feeling as if a slithering snake caressed her. When he pinched her, she cried out.

Georges face grew harsh. "Cotton should've died on the chain gang. Just another nigger dead and gone," he replied bitterly.

Simone could no longer hold back her tears. His words stung her soul. An image of Cotton's handsome face flashed through her mind and she choked back a sob.

At the sight of her tears, Georges face grew lax and he ran a tongue over his lips. "Lay down."

By the time she made it to the bed, tears blurred her vision. On her back, she closed her eyes, fought the urge to sob because Georges' clothes slid from his body. The bed groaned under his weight as he settled his body over her. While he worked to enter her, she took deep breaths, told herself that it would soon be over.

When he grunted, she couldn't help but open her eyes and her stomach did a flip-flop at the sight of him all slack-jawed and humping at her with vigor. "Don't come inside me, Georges. I don't wanna get pregnant," she pleaded.

He groaned, wide mouthed, his face fixed in pleasure. "Move your hips," he moaned, voice trembling.

A sharp intake of breath startled them both and Simone cowered beneath Georges in an attempt to hide herself from Paul's view.

"Shut the damn door," Georges screamed, holding Simone beneath him when she tried to scoot away.

"Sorry, suh," Paul said. He sat a plate of food on a chair near the door then shuffled from the room.

Berta! Would Paul tell?

"I can't," Simone said, squirming from beneath Georges and jumping to her feet.

She snatched her dress from the floor and pulled it over her head. She had to talk to Paul before he found Berta. *Would he tell?*

A blinding pain between her shoulder blades brought her to her knees. An excruciating pain at the back of her head pushed her over the brink into darkness.

~***~

The only light came from a nearby window – from stars glimmering in the night sky. The sun had set long ago.

She was groggy. Her head pounded and she could hardly breathe. When her mind finally cleared, she realized that someone lay atop her – their skin glued to her own by a moisture that revolted her to gagging.

Georges moaned in protest when she pushed at him then finally succeeded in rolling him off of her. She felt his body stiffen – knew that he was awake. A flood of tears finally broke the dam and she sobbed because of the smell of him on her skin, because of the uncomfortable wetness between her thighs and the lingering sensation of him inside of her.

"You raped me," she cried with despair.

Georges turned over and brought his face near to hers until their noses touched. "You wanted it."

She swallowed pain. Desperation made her swallow anger. "At least tell me where he is."

Georges chuckled and turned over onto his back. His tone was honest. "Hell if I know."

~***~

Several weeks came and went with no word from Cotton. Secret ventures to the hills yielded little to no information. Larry and Earl – even Cotton – were presumed dead and Doreen had suspiciously disappeared. Rumors around the hills speculated that Doreen knew all along where the loot was hidden; that the woman set her husband up.

Daisy's bar was now vacant – a mere shell of its former self ruined by a firebomb which everyone assumed served as retribution, warning, and threat.

For Simone, it was that event which brought on the feeling – a welcomed numbness – a sensation that began at her feet and traveled throughout her body to settle into the miserable spaces in her soul – a comforting wall between herself and anguish. When the wall fell, despair settled over her one heavy layer at a time until she felt weighed down by it – on some days exhausted even – until her bedroom became a refuge – a safe haven where she was able to escape the outside world and indulge depression – a tangible dark cloud that settled above her and drowned her in tears. She had not been to the Adrieux plantation since fleeing Georges. On an occasion soon after, Berta invited Paul inside for coffee and she avoided him and his accusatory gaze. If Berta noticed the difference in her behavior, she didn't mention it.

Unfortunately, Georges soon took Paul's place – bringing Berta home by car a few times before making an excuse to come inside the house. To avoid Georges was out of the question – Berta thought her rude to ignore him and would not tolerate Simone's absence especially when Georges asked after her, and Simone would be forced to endure his company in constant panic that Berta would leave the room. At times, he would bring her flowers and Berta would gush that the mayor's son wished to court her daughter. When Berta was away working, he would drive by, passing the house and throwing out a wave if he caught her sweeping the porch or walking from a nearby neighbor's.

At night she dreamt of him – woke up in a cold sweat searching the room for him with panicked eyes. During the day, she kept near the house because her stomach curled in knots at the thought of him catching her out on the road all alone. More than anything she wanted to fill the space with the time that had been lost that terrible day – the lost time where Georges welcomed himself to her unconscious body.

The constant sight of him in and around her home soon turned her depression to debilitating grief, and she would spend her days staring absentmindedly at her bedroom wall with her thoughts torn between Cotton and Georges and the love she felt for one which equaled her hatred for the other. She would rouse herself just hours before Berta was to return home and remove her wrinkled gown to wash and don clean clothes before preparing dinner.

Now she sat in the closet of her bedroom in a far corner and wept. With her head resting on her knees, she rocked back and forth and wiped silent tears from her cheeks with the back of a nervous hand. As far as she was concerned, her life was over.

Once she accepted the fact that Cotton was more than likely dead, she would let herself wonder who her child's father was.

CHAPTER SEVEN

"If you know where that damn boy is, you had better say it this instant!" Maureen stomped a foot and stood stiff-backed with her hands balled into tight fists at her sides.

Simone should have known that there would be trouble when Paul showed up at the house. She was sweeping the porch when the cart pulled up just outside the gate.

"Your mam done sent me 'long to fetch ya," was all he said before turning and staring straight ahead, back rigid, reins clenched tightly in his hands.

Her stomach felt heavy – as if it were poured with cement – and she licked her lips with a dry tongue before asking him what the matter was. He continued to stare straight ahead as if she existed in his mind as only an errand. Her brain instantly jumped to conclusions.

Had Georges said something? Would he be there?

Anxiety caused her to chew her tongue. Her first instinct was to run.

Again the swirling current of the river beckoned to her – tempted her to plunge into its cold depths where she would descend into darkness. The urge to jump had of late become almost overwhelming. In her mind, she saw herself standing at the river's edge, one foot hung out over the water, her body teeter-tottering until she lost her balance and fell headlong...

Now as she stood on the concrete near the walkway of Maureen's garden, she felt as if there was a building perched on her shoulders and she stared at the ground, only gagging slightly when a small pool of brown liquid began to form near her feet. She closed her eyes when a wave of nausea washed over her. When she finally lifted her eyes to meet the sheriff's pale, gray glare, he nodded with satisfaction at her long awaited acknowledgement and turned to pace the edges of Maureen's lush green lawn with his thumbs hooked into his belt.

"Are you drunk?" he asked, pausing to peer into her face.

He was tall and broad shouldered. He stood a good two feet over her and provided shade. The wide brim of his hat blocked out the sun. The weathered skin of his face was flushed a deep red and beneath the brim of his hat, thick blonde brows drew together in a frown. His pupils dilated and made her feel as if she were being studied by the keen eyes of an eagle. There were times that she saw him in and around Woodford County. She had never spoken to him before, but he was intimidating up close – not so much at a distance.

Simone shook her head and her eyes again fell tiredly to her feet. "I'm not feelin' well is all," she whispered.

The worn leather of his boots were layered with a fine sheet of Potluck dust. A slight breeze carried the aroma of tobacco and aftershave. Though she could not see past Sheriff Bradford, she could hear Maureen mumbling bitterly behind him.

"Gal, don't you bullshit me." His tone was calm but threatening. A sudden spray of tobacco juice splattered

Maureen's daisies. "I been out here talking to your mama and the mayor's wife and I know you and that Neal boy is lovey-dovey. Now where is he?"

Berta stood on the porch stone-faced. Her shoulders were slumped with shame.

Simone's heart fell even further but she found her voice. "I don't know where he is, sir. I haven't seen him."

The sheriff's smile caught her off guard. The corners of his eyes crinkled with amusement. He watched her for several seconds – looked her over with a lazy gaze. "There's a story going 'round that he done murdered a man. You understand that?"

Simone nodded and blinked back tears.

She again avoided looking at him – concentrated on her feet – but his eyes bore holes into her. She took a step back to avoid standing with him toe to toe.

"Come on now, gal. That dead man had family and friends. They catch up with that boy 'fore I do and he is dead meat. You understand?"

She lifted her eyes enough to watch his Adam's apple bob as he spit. "I swear I haven't seen him." When she finally forced herself to meet his eyes, they were hard as granite.

"That right?" His voice dropped to a whisper. "What about the murder?"

And her heart skipped a beat. *What would he say?* "What murder?"

Behind them, Maureen gasped.

"Seems Cotton Neal done robbed Harley Roy and murdered him," he said.

"My word!" Maureen exclaimed.

He spoke over his shoulder though his eyes remained on her. "Had three accomplices – one a woman."

"Oh, Simone," Berta groaned.

"You wouldn't know anything about that, now would you, gal?"

Did he think that she – "I ain't killed nobody, sir." The sound of rushing river water beckoned to her.

His tone dropped to a menacing whisper. "If I find out

you're lyin', to me, gal, me and you gonna have a problem. You understand?"

Simone was nodding before he finished his sentence. She bit back tears. His gaze burned through her for several moments before he turned to Maureen and tipped his hat.

As he walked away, Maureen called out behind him. "Good day, Sheriff."

After he climbed into his car, Berta turned without a word and retreated into the house. Simone wanted to run after her mother and apologize but she knew Maureen would refuse to let her into the house. Even now she stood guard near the porch staring at her with judgmental, spiteful eyes.

"Get off my land this instant." Maureen turned to look over her shoulder for Berta. "Shoo."

"Come on, honey," Paul said, limping forward. "I reckon I'll carry ya home."

"The hell you will." Maureen smirked. She stared at Simone with knowing eyes. "She's looking a little round in the face. Maybe she should walk."

Refusing to allow Maureen the pleasure of seeing her cry, Simone turned without a word and walked away. She preferred to crawl home on her hands and knees than accept anything from Maureen. She would not tell Maureen how badly she wanted to ride in Paul's cart. She would not give the woman the satisfaction of knowing how badly she hurt. She would not say how afraid she was that Georges may be waiting for her just down the road.

Once she made it down the path and away from the house, she waited until she rounded the curve and in the dense coverage of walnut trees, she finally let the tears fall – tears that ran from her eyes in streams and pooled beneath her chin. While she walked, she daydreamed of the river's edge.

Just as her mind urged her to step forward and throw herself into the cold abyss, the sound of Paul's horse and cart snatched her from the river's edge and back into reality.

~***~

"Thou shalt not murder!" Pastor shouted at the top of his lungs.

The air in the church was near suffocating and beads of sweat rolled off his dark forehead to be wiped away by a gleaming white handkerchief.

"Is that not one of the commandments that the Almighty God passed down to the children of Israel?" His voice lowered for effect as he stared out over the congregation with his hands clenched tight to the wooden edges of the pulpit. "Honor thy mother and father. How simple is that?" Pastor exclaimed, shaking his head. "Be obedient to your parents. Submit to your husbands."

Simone was startled by the sight of Sheriff Bradford passing beneath the gold, stained glass windows of the church. His hat was lowered so that she could not see his eyes, but she noticed the tenseness in his shoulders and back. He was an unusual Sunday sight to say the least. She faced forward, her eyes momentarily meeting Pastor's before again turning subconsciously toward the window.

Now there was Georges standing beside the sheriff and speaking with him. Something wasn't right.

Her heart leapt. *Cotton?*

Pastor's voice faded into the background – now dimmed by a loud thudding in her chest and she scolded her heart for jumping for joy.

Why else would Sheriff Bradford be there? Did he expect Cotton to show up there? Had Cotton come for her? Was he alive?

Beads of sweat formed on her forehead and she worried her bottom lip with her teeth. It was all she could do to remain in her seat, but she told herself to calm down. She would call attention to herself if she stood up and left mid-sermon. Georges would surely follow her and if Cotton was where she thought he might be, she didn't want to lead the sheriff to his hiding spot.

She would simply have to wait. If he was somewhere out there, he would find a way to get word to her. She smiled secretly to herself. In this moment, not even the sight of Georges could steal her joy.

What else could it be but Cotton finally come to take her away?

"Another commandment," Pastor spat out like a drill sergeant. His voice rose, bringing her back to the present – thundering through the large church until she felt as if he were standing directly over her head. "*Thou shalt not commit adultery.*"

As if on cue, Maureen turned in her seat and stared directly at her.

"Let's all turn to the Book of Proverbs, 28:17," Pastor said. "I'll wait."

As the ruffling of pages turning cut the air, Simone avoided Pastor's disapproving stare. Instead her eyes remained fixed to the back of her mother's head where she sat beside Maureen near the front of the church.

As the double doors of the cathedral were pulled open, a warm gust of wind signaled that services would soon end. She smelled Sheriff Bradford's aftershave before his shadow fell across her, darkening the white pages of scripture that rested in her lap.

"My parting words to you, little children," Pastor's eyes fixed on her downturned face. "*'A man that doeth violence to the blood of any person shall flee to the pit; let no man stay him.'"*

~***~

Simone stood in her bedroom and listened to the raised voices coming from the rear of the shack. Though she felt trapped, her heart still leapt with joy. Cotton had been spotted at his mother's home that very morning. She'd overheard Sheriff Bradford speaking to Berta after services. He had reason to believe that Cotton might show up searching for her.

At that very moment Sheriff Bradford and another deputy together with Maureen, Georges, and Berta stood not too far from her bedroom window – all colluding together to catch Cotton and throw him in prison...or worse, he would be locked up in the city jail where night would cloak the coming of noose-toting, white ghosts of destruction. Then Mrs. Neal's fears would come to fruition. Cotton would swing from a tree.

She would have no father for her child.

Again her heart began to pound when she heard her mother's voice enter the sitting room accompanied by Maureen and Sheriff Bradford. She had escaped to her bedroom under the guise of changing out of her church dress, but instead she stood at her bedroom window with a brow creased in determination while she struggled to lift the window without eliciting its customary groan. For Cotton to find her, she would have to leave the house. Besides, it was only a matter of time before her mother came looking for her – before Sheriff Bradford, who was determined to wear her down, eventually tricked her into revealing the places where Cotton may be hiding.

A quick poke of her head out the window revealed that no one was about. She landed on her feet and for several seconds squatted there beneath the window and listened for movement while she gathered her courage. In an instant, she took a deep breath and sprinted across her mother's garden. At the back gate she threw the latch in one smooth movement and made her way out onto the road. She did not look back.

~***~

They saw one another at the same time. Nothing separated them but the river and they moved around it and toward one another in a daze. To Simone, it seemed that they could not bridge the gap soon enough.

In a secret, secluded spot within the trees she shouted her happiness when Cotton's smooth face came into view. When she stumbled, he caught her before she fell to the ground. She allowed him to lift her off her feet and carry her to crouch beneath the over hanging leaves of a cypress tree. There they kissed and she ran her hands over his face.

"What happened to you?" she asked, tears of happiness running down her face.

"I missed you," he whispered in a tone filled with

emotion. When he kissed her again, his lips lingered and they breathed in one another.

With their foreheads pressed together they held each other. *He had come back for her.*

Cotton pulled her to her feet. His smile convinced her that everything would be alright, and at that moment she loved him so much and had grieved for him for so long that all she could do was stand and bask in the raw emotion in his eyes. She pushed Georges to the back of her mind.

They had been through too much already. Why ruin their happiness with talk of Georges?

She nodded, smiling through her tears and deciding that her child would do just fine with Cotton as a father. She took both of his large hands in her own and placed them on the growing bulge of her stomach. Cotton's eyes grew wide with surprise.

"You're pregnant?"

At the sound of Georges' voice, she broke out in a sweat that instantly dampened the back of her dress. She looked nervously about for the sheriff – her ears attuned to their surroundings for the heavy footfall of booted feet. She pulled at Cotton's arm – panicked to see that he noticed the dangerous, possessive glint in Georges' eyes. He stared between them with a confused frown creasing his brow when Georges stepped forward and beckoned to her.

"Simone." His eyes held a silent warning.

She wanted to scream at him. *I did what you wanted. Why can't you just leave me alone?* Tears from frustration burned her eyes. "Come on, Cotton." She tried to pull Cotton away but he refused – stood his ground. "Please, baby. We have to go now."

"Now, Simone!" Georges' voice was stern, authoritative, and Cotton was taken aback.

Her eyes danced erratically over the trees and she had an intense urge to flee – so much so that she was desperate because of it. *Why was Cotton being so stubborn?* At any moment she expected Sheriff Bradford to come charging toward them – his tan, weathered face burning red with rage.

"Please baby," she begged, pulling Cotton by the arm though he was like stone.

He gave Georges a sly smile. "Still burns you after all these years, eh? That she wanted me."

Georges threw his head back and laughed, finally triumphant, and Simone's eyes fell closed with dread. *No, Georges. Please.* Her legs quivered beneath her. "Cotton."

"Do you want to tell him or should I?" Georges asked her spitefully.

No, please! She had to tell him first.

Cotton shrugged. "Tell me what?"

Simone fell to her knees. "Georges. Please," she stammered, feeling as if the sky was falling atop her. The metallic taste of blood in her mouth did not rescue her bottom lip. She continued to chew the soft flesh while anxiety overwhelmed her. *You set him up.* She wanted to scream. She wanted to tear his eyes out. She wanted to kill him. *You fucking bastard.*

"I never could understand you, man." Cotton shook his head. His eyes were cold. "You're just so...pretty." The word fell from his lips like venom before he growled, giving Georges a hard shove.

Georges staggered back several steps before regaining his balance. He did not retaliate but smiled secretively. His eyes rested on the ground. He pushed a stray lock of hair back from his forehead and snickered quietly before whispering, "Just one more nigger hanging from a tree..."

Cotton's fist fell hard across his face and Georges sunk to his knees, his hands cupping his nose. When Cotton moved toward him he flinched – shielded his head with his arms.

Simone staggered to her feet. "Cotton, baby, let's go." She was so afraid that she felt as if she might faint.

"I'm sorry." Georges stumbled to his feet and wiped blood from his nose with the tail of his shirt. "It's just that she loves you so much." Georges' gaze rested on her. "You have no idea."

Cotton jabbed a threatening finger into his chest. "Stay away from us."

When Cotton turned away, Georges spoke to her through gritted teeth. "You aren't gonna pass that baby along as his, are you?"

Cotton paused and turned. "What?"

"Don't listen to him," Simone begged, now frantic. "He's a liar, Cotton." She grabbed his face in her hands and made him look her in the eye. "You know that." In confusion, Cotton turned again to face a smirking Georges, but Simone stepped in front of him. "Baby, listen to me. We have to get out of here."

"Do you know how desperate she was looking for you while you hid underground with the rest of the rodents?" Georges rocked smugly on the balls of his feet. "Do you know what she did for you – to keep you safe, Cotton?"

"What is he talking about?" Cotton looked down at her, but in his eyes she saw that he already knew. "What happened while I was gone?" he asked, pulling her roughly to him.

"There were a lot of people looking for you," Georges continued. "There was money on your head."

"What is he talking about?" His expression was pained – embarrassed.

"He was gonna tell," Simone choked.

As if struck by lightning, he jumped back from her and his eyes fell to her stomach. "Simone?"

"Oh, no. You don't owe me any thanks." Georges' eyebrows rose suggestively. "She squared up with me. That you can believe."

Cotton turned on her with a snarl and her heart sank into her stomach. His eyes were clouded with pain.

"I did it for you," she cried. "They would've killed you. I had to." She wiped tears from her face. He stared at her as if they were strangers. "He took advantage of me, Cotton." She paused as the words caught in her throat before spilling out. "It was only supposed to be the once but he knocked –"

Before the words could pass her lips, Cotton charged Georges with a roar and knocked him to the ground and as Georges lay beneath him screaming, Cotton pummeled him with his fists before leaping to his feet and stomping Georges in the ribs and face. One last hard boot to the head knocked him out cold.

Together they ran – her hand enclosed tightly in his own while they tore a path through the trees. For several minutes they ran until they reached the back roads where the black iron of railroad tracks led them away from Potluck. Once they reached the Muddy Trail – a back way into the hills only known by its residents – they hid within the foliage like fugitives while Cotton discreetly searched for any movement – any sound – any danger. When nothing stirred, they ran at full speed down the trail making it near a good two miles before Cotton began to whoop with excitement – them both grinning against the adrenaline that pumped through their veins at the expectation of freedom.

At the end of the trail, they abandoned all caution

and happily sprinted out into the clearing. Simone laughed gleefully when Cotton picked her up and swung her around before setting her back on her feet.

~***~

On the other side of the clearing, Sheriff Bradford stepped out of the trees and watched the young couple celebrate their get away – both oblivious to his presence. By habit, the stock of his rifle rose to rest against his shoulder. He squinted with his target eye and leveled his sight on Cotton's chest. The girl was the first to see him. She became so frightened that she stumbled and fell backwards to collide face first with the ground.

"Put your damn hands up!" Marshal screamed.

Cotton's step faltered. *Simone*. He and the sheriff glared at one another.

He turned and threw his arms into the air. His eyes fell to Simone where she lay panting on the ground. She violently shook her head while tears flooded her cheeks. His eyes were filled with sadness; his smile was grave. She knew what he was thinking.

"I love you, Simone," he said and took a step away from her.

"On the ground!"

"Don't, Cotton," Simone screamed.

Cotton circled around and sprinted back toward the trees.

"Cotton! No!"

CHAPTER EIGHT

"Don't you cry for that boy." Berta's tone was filled with disgust.

"And to think that Mayor Adrieux actually set aside important mayoral business in order to deal with this whole terrible mess." Maureen angrily paced the floor with her bible clenched in one pale fist. "Poor Georges." She choked back a sob. "To take a beating from that vicious dog."

Fury burned in Simone's stomach. *He's dead!* She wanted to scream at Maureen. She wanted to tear her hair out. *He's dead you fuckin' bitch!*

"Maureen, I can't begin to tell you how sorry I am," Berta apologized.

Maureen glared at her. "What you should be sorry about is your daughter's reputation." She stared Berta down. "You poor woman. I do believe that your daughter is ruined."

Simone sat on the edge of Maureen's favorite antique high back chair. The smell of floor polish burned her nostrils. She rocked with her hands pressed to her stomach. The sight of Cotton lying dead in the grass, his blank stare attached to the sun – Sheriff Bradford's satisfied smile as he straightened Cotton's neck with the sole of a muddy, leather boot...

"Rancid bitch," she whispered fiercely.

Berta and Maureen gasped simultaneously – the sound similar to the howling of wind.

Maureen rounded on her with clenched fists. "What did you say?"

"Reckon I may as well run you on home now." Paul appeared seemingly from thin air and crossed the room with his steady but uneven gait and headed straight for her. "Come on here, chile." He grabbed her by the elbow and carefully pulled her to her feet.

"What did you call me?" Maureen shouted shrilly. Her face was flushed rage purple.

"I called you a self-righteous bitch." Simone's words dripped resentment. Berta groaned with disappointment.

"Oh, Lawd," Paul sighed and ran a nervous hand across his brow.

Maureen's tone was wicked. "Berta did you know that your daughter was pregnant?"

Berta slumped into a chair and began to cry into her apron.

"But how could you not?" Maureen folded her arms across her chest and eyed Simone with contempt. "She's just so pleasantly plump."

A heavy sigh from Paul was followed by a long groan as he settled into a chair. Simone was now the one to eye Maureen with contempt. She was so humiliated that she could hardly form words. "Your son – rutting, nasty pervert that he is – knocked me out cold so he could climb on top of me."

"Oh my word," Berta exclaimed and grabbed her bosom.

"*You lie!*" Maureen screamed. Her bible fell to the floor with a loud thump and thin lips rolled back to expose her teeth. A large vein pulsed in her forehead *"Don't you accuse my son of that – that bastard child!"* She pointed at Simone's stomach with a shaky finger. *"Everyone knows that you were spreading your legs for Cotton Neal!"*

Simone took a menacing step forward. She wanted to bash Maureen's head in. "He raped me!"

"Oh, help me, Lawd. Help me," Berta cried, her voice breaking with grief.

"Wait a minute now," Paul said shaking his head. "Naw, Ms. Simone. I seen you two wit' my own eyes now. I seen you."

Simone whipped around to face Paul. "You didn't see what happened after you left. When I changed my mind he knocked me out, Paul." She could not stop the flood of tears. She turned on Maureen with her teeth bared. "When I finally came to myself, he was damn near stuck to me."

"Ah. I see," Maureen's eyes narrowed. "The two of you were fornicating in my house and Paul caught you so now you wanna cry rape."

Now exasperated, Paul's head rested in his hands.

"You were always so provocative with Georges – always throwing your tail in his face." Maureen's eyes glittered with malice. "Don't you think for one moment that I'll allow you to ruin my family's good name. " She started again to pace the floor - nearly burned a hole in the carpet. "I'm warning you - if you ever try to hurt my family with your evil lying tongue, I will make it known in Woodford County that you are a whore."

~***~

"I'm so disappointed in you," Berta said. She sat at home in Jeremiah's old chair and sobbed into her hands.

Simone did not speak. It was too much work even for her to breathe. For months, she had kept the incident with Georges to herself feeling as if she had suffered by her own fault, but now that Cotton was dead – now that she was pregnant and unwed – the scandal of Potluck, she wanted to go to County Hospital where Cotton now lay and murder him.

Berta's gaze was incredulous. Her fat, dark cheeks shone with tears. "What is wrong with you, Simone? What is wrong with you?"

Simone gasped for air because she felt as if she were suffocating.

"Didn't I tell you that boy was gonna 'cause you trouble?" Berta's voice rose with restrained ire. "Didn't I?"

Simone closed her eyes against an ache which slowly spread throughout her chest. With Cotton gone, she felt as if her life was over.

But for her, there was always the river. For Berta, there was nothing but disgrace. Her once sanctimonious household was now the gossip of the community. Maureen's once pious household would be scrutinized because of the actions of Berta's only child.

"And Georges?" Berta shook her head in disbelief. She was stunned. "I known that boy most of his life. How could you lie on him like that? How?"

Simone's mind wandered again to the rushing river –

its cold depths called her by name.

"You ought to thank that young man for saving your life – for putting his own reputation on the line and stepping up to marry you." Berta scowled at her. "Hell, for all he knows the child probably ain't even his. And goodness knows that me and your daddy didn't raise you like that." Berta's nose curled with disgust. "Lay down with dogs and you catch fleas. You should be ashamed of yourself."

The insult to Cotton pushed Simone over the edge. "I'm so tired of you kissing Adrieux ass." She could no longer control herself.

Berta met her anger. "You didn't care about that when Maureen gave you all those fancy ass French books." Berta gave her a dismissive wave. "But you don't appreciate shit. When your daddy got sick and Raymond Adrieux paid for his hospital -

"So what!" Simone screamed hysterically.

Berta slowly rose from the chair. "I want you out of my house."

With that Simone's heart broke. She could not depend on her own mother for support.

She fled the house only to collapse on the porch. Her tortured screams tore through the night.

~***~

For two Sundays in a row, Berta skipped church. She was humiliated beyond speaking, hardly wanted to be seen and would not accept visitors because of the sordid details of Cotton's death and circulating rumors of sexual indiscretion involving Simone and Georges Adrieux. Simone had never seen her mother so low.

As for herself, she could care less. As far as she was concerned, there was nothing left for her to live for.

On the third Sunday, Berta rapped lightly at Simone's bedroom door and told her she had ten minutes to prepare for a trip to the general store.

Their walk together – something in the past that they had both enjoyed before Berta broke her leg – was now strained and awkward for them both. Simone attempted to draw her mother into conversation but Berta simply ignored her – enforcing the fact that she was no longer welcome in her childhood home. Georges made it clear to Berta that he wanted to marry Simone though she refused to talk to him. Georges was the only subject her mother would talk with her about.

Berta shamefully bowed her head when the conversations of those loitering around the store suddenly ceased. Simone followed her mother up the steps, cringing at the whispers which met her ears.

"She was doin' him and the Neal boy?"

"Yep."

"At the same time?"

A hearty groan. "Those poor guys."

Simone's pace slowed while Berta disappeared into the store behind the chiming of an overhead bell.

"Boy, you betta watch your mouth, Joe." Chuckle, chuckle.

Simone pulled the door open and entered the store,

closing off the voices behind her only to be surrounded by an unpleasant tension as the usually talkative customers of the general store fell silent at her entry. Berta cowered at the back of the store – busied herself with scooping flour from a bin.

Hushed, accusatory grumbling followed her.

"I'll bet her tail is on fire. Ain't like she never did it before."

"Humph."

"I'm telling you she wasn't no virgin..."

"No good harlot."

"...oughtta snatch her bald. Little lyin..."

She reached out a hand to help Berta with the armful of goods that she held, but Berta turned away from her and approached the counter with a smile meant for the cashier. Once their purchases were tabbed, Berta fled the store with her head down and left Simone to carry the packages alone.

Knowing what awaited her outside, she took a deep breath and exited the store behind her mother. She ignored the demeaning glares of two women who she was forced to sidestep as they passed her on the stairs. The fear of imminent degradation made her stumble over her feet.

"To sit up and blame him for raping her after she done tried to run off wit' a dead man. Maureen is a saint."

"I know one thing, she'd betta be glad it wasn't my son or I would've went upside her head. Little tramp."

"And he wants to marry her. Can you believe it?"

Simone bit her lip and blinked back tears. As best she could, she managed to carry the packages by balancing them atop her bulging stomach. She stared longingly at her mother's retreating back and yearned for comfort.

~***~

Two months before Simone was set to deliver her baby, Maureen Adrieux traveled one county past Woodford and purchased a home in the country for Georges and his new wife whom Berta gladly married off. She was more concerned with restoring her own reputation now that her pregnant daughter was married to the mayor's son.

Neither Berta nor an Adrieux ever visited the couple.

Though there was no music, Georges lifted her off her feet, molding her body to his own, and danced with her to a tune he hummed from deep within his throat. He spun her in an endless circle across the parlor floor until she was too dizzy to stand. When he lowered her to the floor and removed her cloak, the child in her stomach balled into a knot. She swallowed the urge to vomit when his dry lips found the base of her throat.

As the sun set and he moved within her, Simone cried for Cotton silent tears. The thought of her mother's betrayal stung like a dozen knives to her heart. The sound of her heart breaking was like the splintering of glass.

Georges moaned, grinding his hips into her own. The glass broke, burst into a million tiny shards – the fracture an audible shattering in her ears.

This night was different than any other. This night she finally got away and even though she knew that dogs could swim, her intent was to make it to the river and drown herself before he could catch up with her. That was the only way she would ever be free of him.

How she had made it so far, so fast she could not remember, but when she made it to the road, she did not stop and her slim legs pumped ferociously as she went and she ignored the blood that flowed freely from the large wound in her arm. She clutched a hand over her large belly, feeling the baby stretching – moving inside of her.

Her senses were so taut that she could see in the dark. She was so afraid that she needed no light to guide her. She was being pursued, chased down by a hungry, humping monster. The wind tore through the thin, ripped fabric of her gown and cooled her skin.

Moments later, she was gone.

PART TWO

Through dimming eyes, Ines watched the beautiful young woman seated across from her for as long as she could.

With a weak arm she reached for her only child – palm facing skyward, mouth awkwardly agape – when the first spasm hit. Before darkness fell, she exhaled one last suffocating breath just as her fingers were enclosed in the comforting warmth of Antoinette's trembling hands.

Toni took hold of the moist hand offered to her, the palm turned outward, thumb and index finger cupped protectively around a silver key, and when she pocketed it, she reminded herself that taking it wasn't the same as stealing. You couldn't steal what already belonged to you.

She kneeled beside her mother's chair and brushed a kiss over her damp forehead then in exhaustion and grief her head fell and came to rest on their intertwined fingers. A lone tear fell from her eye, struck a path across the bridge of her nose before moving on to pool between her nostrils and falling with a quiet plop to the porch. She had not expected the sudden stillness – the absence of labored breathing – a sound that she had become surprisingly accustomed to the last weeks of her mother's life. It was not the dying that bothered Toni. It was the waiting – waiting while her mother suffered.

She did not shed another tear. She ably admitted to herself the relief she felt for not having to spend another night at her mother's bedside waiting – waiting while she died. But now she was all too aware of a silence that was broken only by the wispy buzz of mosquitos and the steady, remorseful wailing of cicadas.

A fragrant, flowery breeze passed through the porch screen to cool her sweat dampened skin and the wet trail that one lone tear left behind. Several minutes passed before she gently tucked Ines' hands beneath the red patchwork quilt, pulling the edges of the blanket up around her thin shoulders and tucking the fabric beneath her chin as if she still ran the risk of catching a chill. She allowed her hand to linger at her mother's cheek and was wholly aware of the stillness – the lack of electricity – of life.

When she finally traveled across the porch, she did so in a daze, only pausing once to glance over her shoulder at her mother because she half expected her to call her back.

Ines merely sat motionless in her chair and with blind eyes stared blankly out at the road.

CHAPTER ONE

Toussaint, Louisiana 1957

It came as no great shock when Eugene Baptiste married Stella Monroe – not because his late wife, Ines, was not yet cold in her grave, but because it was an openly known fact that Stella and Eugene were having an affair.

Ines and Stella were polar opposites. Ines had been a meek, country-bred woman, tan with long, brown hair and a swatch of freckles that covered her entire face. She had been petite – bony even – pretty enough to be called attractive, but not nearly as much as Stella who was voluptuously buxom, sassy and dark-skinned with striking hazel eyes and a full mouth.

Ines had been a homebody, preferring to attend ladies' events and church meetings in hat and white gloves while no one would ever believe that Stella would step foot in the house of prayer – especially when there was a pool hall so close nearby. Besides, in all likelihood she would probably be throttled the moment she placed her full bottom in a pew because she made it her business to sleep with any married man willing to slide between her smooth, brown thighs.

The women of Toussaint empathized with Ines when her turn came about – not because Eugene decided to make time with the town Jezebel, but because he lingered where most men only desired to rest their hat for a short while. And when Ines became ill, Eugene abandoned sensitivity and took up with Stella out in the open, flaunting their relationship as if his wife were irrelevant with rumor having it that he was simply counting the money – which was no surprise.

In ladies' circles they concentrated on assumption…

Eugene married Ines for her inheritance and because she tolerated his womanizing, the whiskey, losing all her money at the pool hall…

While sitting on fancy lawn chairs and sipping iced tea beneath the warm rays of a Louisiana sun their tongues gossiped unabashedly – bored housewives musing contentedly that she had gone the way of many other desperate women who preceded her. And such a shame too since Ines was still a young woman of only forty-five when she passed.

But that's what happens when you get hitched to a low down, dirty cheater. Cluck, cluck…What a shame, shame!

Embarrassing even that when she was terribly sick and clinging to life she still was not loved by the only man that she had ever wanted.

But really…did desperation make her believe that her im-pend-ing death would soften his heart toward her? Well, cluck, cluck…when the reaper found her porch, old Eugene kicked her butt straight out the door. That po' chile married a rattlesnake.

Sorry sucka…

And the girl…

Antoinette?

Mm-hmm. Can you imagine watching your mama spit up blood and knowing your daddy can't even spell 'discretion'.

I tell you, my Mitchell ain't perfect, but to have to compete with the likes of Stella Monroe for the whole world to see? Oooh, my word.

Girl, stop. You know how long he been creeping on that kitty?

Cluck, cluck...

But such is the path for women who dangle wealth to catch a mate. And so Toussaint knew full well that Eugene waited with his mistress while Ines died on the porch.

In late summer of '57, just two months after Ines Baptiste was laid to rest, Stella Monroe and her twenty-six year old daughter, Delphine, came to live permanently in the Baptiste home. Toni at that time, still mourning her mother's death, was outraged with her father.

As for Stella, Toni could not help but be curious. What sort of woman could ignore the stares – the whispers? Would a decent woman marry a widower so soon after his wife's death? She stood at the parlor window with her eyes glued to the strange woman and her daughter not realizing that she held her breath until they stepped out of Eugene's Cadillac and started toward the house with suitcases in tow.

The first thing she noticed was how unlike her mother this new woman was and she exhaled and took a deep breath in effort to control the burning anger that swelled in her chest.

While she watched her sashay up the walk, Toni was not conscious of the vicious curl of her own upper lip or the sting of her nails biting into her palms. Her eyes remained on the curvaceous figure in black stilettos and crimson dress – a dress her mother would never have worn – a dress that clung to Stella's body like a second skin. Toni frowned because of the short, soft curls that framed the woman's lovely face, the baby doll brown eyes framed by faux lashes, the too red lips – but lastly, the way that she hung over Eugene without shame and the way that he allowed it, grinning broadly from ear to ear with one arm surrounding Stella's small waist with a too sudden familiarity. Toni tried to recall a time where she had ever seen him hold her mother that way.

Dramatic from the start, Stella stepped over the threshold and into Ines' spotless home and excitedly clapped her hands together while she took in the spacious interior with insincere awe. "Oh, Eugene! It's beautiful."

Stella ignored her but Delphine watched her with apt interest. The young woman, like her mother, possessed velvety dark skin and overwhelmingly beautiful eyes and for some time, Delphine and Toni appraised one another with glares filled with challenge. This non-verbal exchange amused Stella who held Eugene on a leash while watching them with the wicked gaze of a chronic instigator. When the silence between the two young women became tense, she interrupted.

"And this, Eugene?" she asked, gesturing to Toni with a flick of a red fingernail.

Eugene walked over and placed a heavy hand on Toni's shoulder. "This here my baby girl, Toni." Though he addressed her, he avoided eye contact. "Toni, this here is

Stella, my wife."

Toni shrugged Eugene's hand from her shoulder and turned to stare him in the face, gritting her teeth to hold her tongue in check because he refused to look at her though an embarrassed twitch of his jaw told her that he avoided looking at her because he knew how wrong he was.

She stormed past Stella who was delighted at her discomfort. Delphine's mocking, high-pitched laughter chased her from the house.

~***~

It began with small things – Stella gradually, little by little, changing the home until any hint of Ines disappeared from sight. When Antoinette fought for her mother, Stella would retaliate by wearing Ines' jewelry. When Eugene refused to intervene on his daughter's behalf, Stella went a step further – eventually dropping subtle insults about the dead to test the waters. The meanness came and went as suddenly as Toni disappeared or re-appeared in a room – Stella determined to find a way to pierce her heart.

Consequences of the last straw were provoked –
Stella wearing Ines' favorite brooch. A brooch that Toni
purposely hidden in her very own jewelry box – a keepsake
that she kept to remember her mother by.

"Give it back," Toni spat, reaching out to tear the
jewel from Stella's blouse.

"Get your silly ass off of me!" Stella cried. She had not
been expecting a physical attack. "Eugene!"

The first slap echoed through the house and left
Stella slack jawed with a trembling hand pressed to her face,
but when Toni smiled at her, her face twisted into a sneer,
she came at her with nails curled into claws. The first swing
tore skin from Toni's cheek, leaving a sting that brought
with it an instant rush of mad rage that flowed through her
like molten lava. With a scream akin to a war cry, she
attacked Stella, growling her satisfaction when the woman
yelped – grunting with pleasure when the hard sole of her
shoe scraped the length of Stella's shin and elicited another
frightened cry for her husband.

Eugene appeared ragged and red-eyed, ornery and mean from a night spent working for debauchery. His eyes widened when he realized that the women were engrossed in battle – both swinging and missing, punching and connecting, cursing and spitting.

"What the hell!" he thundered before rushing into the midst of combat to tear them apart. He soon realized his mistake as Toni's fists and feet pummeled him and Stella's long, false fingernails slashed his face. Now trapped between them, he was collateral damage.

"You silly little bitch!" Stella screamed from behind Eugene's broad back.

While Eugene acted as a shield for his wife, Toni angrily paced the floor like a vicious, caged animal.

"Don't you ever put your nasty home wrecking hands on anything of my mother's!"

"She ain't hurting your momma none." Eugene glared at her. "What you guarding?"

Toni pointed an accusing finger at him. "You couldn't

even wait," she screamed. Tears of frustration brimmed in her eyes.

Eugene suddenly looked exhausted. "You're a grown woman, Toni."

She shook her head at him. "She's wearing my mother's brooch. Tell her to give it to me."

"She is disrespectful. And violent," Stella screamed, taking the high road. "I see now that I have to defend myself in my own house!"

When Toni advanced toward her, Eugene grabbed her by the shoulders. "You kick this woman, girl?" Eugene asked.

"And smacked me," Stella added. "And don't you dare stand there and lie through your teeth." Stella sat at the table, enjoying Eugene's stupidity. "This had to have been one spoilt child," she said.

"Shut up, cow," Toni said. She fought the urge to wrench free of Eugene and slap her.

"*Antoinette!*" Eugene exclaimed.

"Spare the rod, hurt the child," Stella continued. "I am telling you that she attacked me like some kind of wild animal." She pouted when Eugene moved to comfort her. "You saw her. I don't know what I would've done if you hadn't been here."

Toni's eyebrows rose at Stella's dramatically smug, flawless act. Eugene's dark face was handsome but hard. Toni was not surprised at the callous look in his eyes. It was the same look that he gave her mother – the one that flitted over her without remorse or apology.

"I ain't never known her to lie," he said to Stella, "but she jealous. Just lost her mama, that's why she showing out."

"Showing out," Stella exclaimed. "This here ain't no little girl no more, Eugene."

Tears threatened to overflow but she refused to let Stella see her cry. Stella who behind Eugene's back often watched her with beautiful eyes that glittered with envy.

She passed the two of them with downcast eyes and fought the urge to clobber Stella and tear the brooch from her blouse.

Eugene's voice was loud behind her. "If you don't like what goes on in this house, girl, the front door open same way it close."

~***~

She sat on a gigantic, rotting log and concentrated on the slapping of waves and squawking of gulls, on the river scented breeze that blew through her hair and cooled her scalp.

She thought about her mother's key – *her key.*

When Simone moved back home a year before to care for her mother, she was somewhat shocked at the fact that her father rarely came home – rarely looked in on Ines at all. He had never been a loving man but Ines was dying after all.

There were moments when he would briefly appear. He would whisk an ailing Ines away to their bedroom overnight before leaving her in the morning and Toni would find her mother sitting up in bed alone, a wistful smile on her face as she dismissively explained away Toni's confusion with an explanation as simple as he needed papers signed for this thing or the other. Weeks would pass before he would appear out of nowhere for some odd item that he needed for some odd reason. She watched her mother come to the painful realization that he had never loved her.

Daddy Gene.

Though he drank and gambled to an excessive amount, had it just been she and her father, she might have confided in him about the key. But because of Stella she could no longer trust him. The woman had taken over everything – her mother's husband and house.

Toni decided that she would follow Eugene's advice and find another place to live. She had to face the fact that it was time for her to get on with her life. There was no longer a place for her in her mother's home. It was time for her to take what she had and leave.

Toni frowned, rolled her eyes, and forcefully let go of

an irritated breath. At times her river trips were cut short too soon. She could hear Delphine's ragged breathing as she struggled to avoid stepping in mud with her patent leather high heeled sandals.

"Toni! Mama looking for you."

A familiar boil began in her stomach. Several days had passed since the altercation between she and Stella, but she knew it was only a matter of time before the older woman sought revenge.

"She's not my mother." She turned and studied Delphine's face – Delphine who was just a younger version of Stella.

She stood with crossed arms and smirked at Toni's defiance. Her hair was freshly pressed and bounced around her shoulders in soft ringlets. Though she was a few inches shorter than Toni, the fancy shoes gave her more height and accentuated the shapeliness of her legs – legs bared by a skirt that was way too short and a sweater that was way too tight and hugged her curves to a way too sinful degree.

Hazel, cat eyes spoke to her of open dislike and Toni

smirked in response.

"Get down from that broke ass tree and come along.

Like I said, Mama is looking for you."

Delphine turned on her heel and sashayed away.

~***~

"That woman was a sorry excuse for a mother," Stella

looked at Delphine but spoke to Toni. She crossed her arms

and shook her head. "Look how she raised this heifer."

"Stella, now –"

"I'm sorry, Eugene, but the girl is selfish. This is what

happens when you indulge a child."

Toni knew this game.

Stella on a scavenger hunt. Stella searching for any

remaining joy in her with which to stomp out. She stood in

the living room and paced the expensive chenille rug that

Stella had purchased with her mother's money – *her money*

– and kept her head down.

"I would pay the money back in a year," Delphine

whined, gesturing toward Toni with an exasperated hand. "I mean, really?"

Toni paced the floor with her arms crossed so tightly over her chest that her hands were beginning to numb. "That's my money, Daddy Gene," she started out calmly. "Mother left it for me – what's left anyway," she added sarcastically while cutting her eyes in Stella's direction. "When are you going to get around to putting my name on that account?" she added bitterly.

"Girl, stop your complaining." Eugene avoided her question. "Your sister is standing here –"

"She ain't my sister." Toni's tone was final.

Stella and Delphine laughed loudly together.

"*Delphine* is standing here asking you for a loan and you're spitting in her damn face." Eugene's words slurred. "Once she get that hair salon up and running, you'll get the money right back."

"Then why won't you give it to her? How come she can't get it from her own mother?" Toni spat spitefully, ignoring Stella's sharp intake of breath. "No! She wants what my mother gave to me." She wanted to knock the smug look off of Stella's face. "It's mine. I need it so I can get out of this house."

"And good riddance," Stella said haughtily.

"Well, right now I'm in charge of that money and I think this will be good for the family." Eugene rose from his chair with a knowing smile on his face. "Besides, I know your mother left you with something. But you don't wanna talk about that. Right?"

Toni realized then that Eugene never meant to give her one red cent.

His voice was tinged with disdain. "You act just like your sorry ass mama."

CHAPTER TWO

Stella was not in the least bit happy to be mother to her own child let alone be forced to act as stand in mother to the ignorant daughter of her husband and his dead wife – a woman whom Stella had always thought to be weak and terribly plain. In her opinion, any woman that would marry a broke Eugene Baptiste and allow him to run her household was indeed a fool and unworthy of her respect.

Who would have thought that he would ask her to marry him? To say that she was caught off guard when he offered her the ring would be an understatement.

Had she loved him? Did she love him now? Of course not. *But was he a fool to her whim and an excellent provider?* Absolutely.

Had she felt bad? Nope.

Because Ines not only had a handsome husband but she also had a more than decent bank account and a beautiful home. And to Eugene's credit, he was more than generous with her money.

My money. Ice cubes clinked loudly together as she drained the bitter liquid in her glass. She crossed one curvaceous leg over the other and smiled down at the brand new leather pumps that had been purchased with Ines' money. *Her money.*

Stella was very proud of herself. She'd come a long way from that raggedy, shoebox house in the country. But there is where her reputation was born. As she reminisced, her jaw unconsciously clenched.

For many years to support herself she made homemade wine which she sold in corked, glass bottles out of her bedroom window. During the day she slept, but at night she would curl her hair and apply her trademark burgundy lipstick, and from sunset to the wee hours of morn, she would sit prettily with her elbows on the leaning sill of her bedroom window and wait for hand after hand – masculine and feminine, white and black alike – to reach in with crumpled green bills for their pint.

Hadn't she told every mad, vengeful wife that showed

up on her doorstep – *hey honey, your man came to me.* And to Stella, that was all the explanation needed. *'Cause if you can't satisfy your man, I will.*

And that's what she loved about Ines – she never put up a fuss.

At first, Eugene had been for her a joy and she fancied herself in love. He flaunted her around as if he were a single man engaged in a proper courtship and she was more than flattered by his attentions. He was sturdy and rough around the edges, a considerate, aggressive lover who showered her with gifts. He was jealous – chasing all her beaus away with threats of violence. At forty years old, she felt like a girl again.

Stella paced the enclosed porch with a whiskey bottle in her hand. A half melted ice cube broke between her teeth before she melted it with a swig from the bottle. She laughed aloud when her imagination conjured an image of Toni up in her bedroom crying like a baby.

At this very moment lay in Eugene's bottom dresser

drawer the cash needed to make the payment on the small salon in downtown Toussaint. Eugene made the withdrawal just that afternoon. By tomorrow morning, Delphine would be a business owner.

What Eugene didn't know was that in less than a year's time she planned to divorce him. She and Delphine would never again have to worry about making ends meet once the shop was up and running. And she simply wouldn't need him anymore.

And maybe, just maybe, she would leave him with whatever remained of Ines' soon to be depleted bank account.

She cut her eyes toward the house. She was very offended by Toni's presence.

A grown woman living in her daddy's house. Damn shame. But maybe the little bitch finally realized who was boss.

~***~

Toni sat on the floor near her bed and played with

the frayed edges of a faded patchwork quilt. Because she was so nervous, her ears played tricks on her and every few seconds she imagined that she could hear Otis Redding's voice dominating the road and then Eugene's car idling in the driveway.

She took a deep breath and closed her eyes. She was paranoid – that was all. Why would he suddenly come home early on this night when his usual habit was to stay out at the pool hall until the wee hours of morning?

Though she was nervous, she was also excited, and she stared thoughtfully at the waiting branches of an old oak tree that sat just outside her open bedroom window. In her mind, she again took inventory of the things that were important to her – weighed the pros and cons of her next decision.

If she didn't leave now she would be destitute – left by her father's indifference to Stella's wicked form of acting on her jealousy. She had to make a decision now before Eugene and Stella realized that the money was gone.

While a grass scented breeze wafted through the open window, fluttering the white lace curtains that her mother had sewn for her, she examined the key which opened Ines' safety deposit box. One day she would come back to Toussaint to collect the contents.

Could she leave her father alone?

She envisioned Stella unexpectedly leaving the porch where she sat nightly with her whiskey. When semi-drunk, she would leave her liquor and head to bed. But first she would discover that the money had vanished from Eugene's armoire.

Of course, Toni would be the one to blame. She would be penalized for stealing part of her own inheritance. This was definitely not the way she planned on departing her childhood home, but it seemed her only option was to revert to desperate measures.

An open, packed duffel bag sat beneath the window. It was full of things that she absolutely could not live without together with enough clothes to tide her over until she made it west where she planned to start over.

Somewhat dazed, but with her mind made up, she donned her favorite cardigan and grabbed her bag. Without hesitation, she walked to the window, swung her legs over the sill and from habit, expertly grabbed ahold of the large tree and shimmied gracefully down the trunk to jump the remaining few feet to the ground. She landed soundlessly on the grass.

Once she made it across the large yard, she quickened her pace wanting to put as much distance between herself and the house as she could. Though it was dark, she knew the way by heart, and when she made it to the dirt road, she stuffed her hands into her pockets and grinned to herself.

Just when she thought that she would never win opportunity had presented itself in the form of a bank envelope containing fifty crisp green bills. All of which bore the face of Ben Franklin – now her favorite president. Lucky for her, she had just so happened to hear Stella's joyous laughter when Eugene showed her the money.

She cut across Emmett Parsons property at a slow jog. Several minutes later, she made it to County Road 5. Her mind conjured an image of Stella's face when she realized that the money was missing – that she was missing as well. The first thing Stella would do is run down to the pool hall for Eugene who would waste no time searching her out. Lucky for her, she had a head start.

With her bag slung over her shoulder, she waited by the nearest mile marker. Right on time, headlights appeared in the distance.

Toni searched the friendly face of the driver with narrowed eyes. The van he drove was small – a terrible rusted brown metal that vibrated with the grating of the muffler.

A female sat in the passenger seat. She was slender, willowy and light-skinned. Freckles covered her entire face. Her hair was long and wavy and she wore a pair of large hoop earrings. Gold bangles adorned her arms. Her smile was friendly. She resembled Ines.

The driver, handsome and sturdily built, tipped his hat and grinned. Toni smiled in return.

"You sure you wanna leave like this?" the girl asked.

Without answering, Toni slid the van door open and climbed in.

"Where you going?" A male passenger sat in the backseat across from her. He had once tried to court her some years back but she was not attracted to him.

"California, Wardy," she responded.

Fred whistled from the driver's seat. "How in the hell you standing out here trying to go all the way to damn California?"

Toni smiled when he grunted because the pretty girl in the passenger seat punched him in the side with a bony fist.

"How long before you gotta be there?" she asked, turning in her seat.

177

Toni shrugged. "Doesn't matter, Stacy. Just get me outta here."

"Where you gone stay when you get there?"

"I'll be alright."

"I wish you'd come with us for a while."

"Where to?" She should've known that her cousin would get into her business.

"Well, we're headed to Fred's house in Dallas," Stacy said, gum popping. "Come hang with us for a while. It's not like you're in a grand rush and who knows the next time we'll see each other."

While Stacy and Fred sat up front and chatted, Toni sat in the back of the van and stared out the window. Melancholy settled over her and she couldn't shake it.

"Why wouldn't you ever go out with me again?" Wardy whispered. Toni turned to find him leaning over the arm of his seat toward her.

Because you're an octopus, she thought.

Instead she said, "My mother was ill. I had to take care of her."

Which was true, but not totally. Had she been attracted to Wardy?

Toni looked him over with slow eyes. To her, he was too big, stood too tall, was too muscular though his skin was as smooth and dark as polished onyx and his eyes were startling – a deep, piercing black. But he was too clingy – called on her too much, stopping by unannounced and even startling her once by calling Eugene *'Daddy Gene'*. But mostly, it irked her that he always leaned in for a kiss (lips puckered like a dry flower) knowing full well that he didn't have permission to take liberties with her person.

"Well, I want you to know what I see when I look at you," Wardy started, leaning across his seat toward her. "I see you, baby. For you. It's not just that you're beautiful..." Toni tuned his voice out until his lips moved soundlessly. She stared him directly in the face. *Blah, blah, blah.*

But then he reached across the aisle to enclose her

hand in his own.

"...a long-legged beauty the shade of warm honey."
He licked his lips and gave her a flirtatious wink. "Fate
brought us together on this road," he whispered.

"How's it going back there?" Fred called from the
front seat whilst eying them through the rearview mirror.
"You wearing her down, my boy?" he teased.

Wardy released her hand and lifted a middle finger
for Fred to view. Just as Toni rolled her eyes, Stacy fell into a
fit of giggles.

For a change it was quiet inside the van. Stacy's
incessant chattering had ceased and Wardy laid his
harmonica to rest on the seat beside him. The air was now
filled with nervous tension.

They would be stranded.

Despite her complaining, they had all sat inside a
roadside diner for over an hour before sitting for another
hour out in the van with Stacy blasting the radio and

dancing in the parking lot while they passed a joint around. When they'd finally gotten on the road, Toni was convinced that they'd gone in the wrong direction – that somewhere along the way Fred made a wrong turn.

They were now on a dark, tree-lined dirt road. The round glare of the van's headlights illuminated the rich green of Louisiana trees and the glow of small eyes watching them from the brush.

A loud, persistent squealing that started miles back was now accompanied by white clouds of smoke that escaped from beneath the hood of the van. Toni and Fred let out simultaneous groans of disappointment.

"Damn it!" Wardy cursed.

Fred grumbled. "Ain't this about a –"

"Pull over, Fred," Toni said, knowing that they were simply prolonging the inevitable.

"Then what? We're all the way out in the middle of –"

"Just pull over, man," Wardy said. "If we keep going like this it'll only make it worse."

With a jaw set in agitation, Fred reluctantly pulled the van to the edge of the road and shut off the engine.

"Now what are we gonna do?" Stacy pouted while the three of them climbed from the van and left her to bite her nails.

Fred struggled to lift the hood. "Can't see shit out here," he complained, coughing and waving to clear the smoke. "Wardy, you gonna help me out or what?"

"I don't know nothing about cars, man." Wardy shrugged his shoulders and stuffed his hands into his pockets. "Besides, I don't wanna get oil all over me."

Fred looked around the hood at him. "Boy, if you don't -"

"Someone's coming," Toni said, peering at lights approaching from further down the road.

They all turned to stare at the approaching vehicle.

Fred exhaled a relieved breath. "Thank God," he said.

"I don't know," Wardy said. "It's dark. We're black." A few seconds later he added, "You're fat."

"Shut up, Wardy," Toni mumbled.

As they bickered, a wide, red pick-up truck came rambling down the road. When it neared them, it slowed then stopped before the driver leaned out the window and gave them a welcoming smile. They relaxed at the sight of his light brown face.

The second thing Toni noticed about him was how attractive he was and she openly stared in spite of herself then blushed when he gave her a friendly smile. His gaze dropped shyly before rising again and for mere seconds their eyes met and held – both full of poignant interest suddenly interrupted by a loud clearing of Wardy's throat.

"Man, are we glad to see you," he said, though his eyes were on Toni.

"You guys broke down?"

"Yep," Fred replied. "Bad belt."

The red truck pulled to the side of the road and though Toni could feel Wardy's jealous glare burning into the side of her face, her eyes remained on the tall, lean young man who stepped from the truck.

Fred extended a hand and introduced himself. "Fred."

Toni watched the sensual motion of perfect lips forming words and closed her eyes when a rich baritone sent a delicious shiver up her spine. *Olivier.*

When he spoke, it seemed to Toni that a soft wind suddenly blew through the trees then lovingly fondled fallen leaves before reaching up to run sensual fingers through her hair to cool and caress her scalp. She opened her eyes to find Wardy staring at her – a sullen grimace twisted his face.

Still a soft sigh slowly escaped her lips.

Together Olivier and Fred leaned beneath the van's hood to get a better look at the shredded belt and Toni approached them – purposefully sidestepping a glaring Wardy to stand between them though she had no idea what they were talking about.

But she was more than happy to stand and nod like a fool as long as she could continue to catch the occasional, bashful glance from Olivier's big brown eyes. His short

sleeve shirt bared muscled forearms and calloused hands –
and when he caught her watching him, he gave her a
flirtatious smile before lowering his eyes.

"Quite a ways to the next service station. My place is
some miles down the road. I'm pretty sure I got a belt that'll
fit."

"Really?" Fred asked, again relieved. "That would be
great. Listen I'll pay to replace it."

"It's no problem," Olivier waved a hand in dismissal
of Fred's offer. "I got junk lying around all over the place.
You'd be doing me a favor taking it off my hands."

Toni touched his forearm with her fingertips and he
smiled down at her. "Still that's very nice of you to help us."

"Yes," Wardy agreed but frowned in her direction.
"Nice."

Olivier gave her hand a cursory pat before turning
back to Fred. "So why don't we tow it on down to my place."

Together Olivier and Fred secured the van to the
truck. Toni stood at the side of the road watching while

Wardy stood by himself and glowered at Olivier's back.

Together they piled into the truck, Toni climbing into the front seat and happily squeezing in between Olivier and Fred while leaving Wardy to ride behind them in the van with a slumbering Stacy.

They chatted as they drove. Olivier and Fred picked up a friendly conversation about cars which led to a deeper discussion about the restoration of one of Olivier's vehicles – a project that he had started some years back. Toni enjoyed several long minutes of sitting close to Olivier with his hard thigh pressed against her own. After a few miles he turned onto a road which led to a three-story clapboard house. The property was surrounded by a dense, forest like layer of trees with the house sitting in the midst of the green – a beautiful habitation surrounded by windows covered with freshly painted black shutters.

Behind the house, Toni could see a large barn and another smaller structure that she assumed was a storage shed. Beyond the house lay a full field of sunflowers that seemed to sway more than the soft breeze could stir. They reached skyward as if impatiently waiting for the first rays of sun from the twi-lit sky. In their midst was a gazebo surrounded by a small, circular pond.

"So this is your place, huh?" Fred asked.

Olivier nodded. "Yep. Lived here all my life."

The truck came to rest in front of the house and Olivier climbed from the driver's seat then turned and offered Toni a dramatic bow followed by a gallant arm for aid and she laughed with him and gave him her hand. When she slid to the edge of the seat, he wrapped strong hands around her waist and lifted her into his arms. Toni hardly noticed a groggy Stacy or a frowning Wardy or even Fred who grinned like a Cheshire cat.

"You mind if we look around?" Wardy asked a little too loudly.

Olivier placed her on her feet and winked at her before turning to Wardy. His tone was cool. "I figured you'd wanna come back and help me and Fred find this belt, man."

Wardy shook his head. "No, I figured Toni might wanna take a walk in the garden. Toni?"

"No," Toni said, shaking her head. "I think I'll go help them find that belt. How about you and Stacy hang out by the truck and we'll –"

The sudden, loud barking of a dog startled her into speechlessness. The shed seemed to shudder of its own accord.

Stacy was instantly wakeful. "That your dog?" she asked Olivier, eyes wide with fright.

"Don't you worry about him," he reassured her. "He's locked up."

"We'll stay here," Wardy grumbled.

After helping Fred and Olivier push the van into the garage, Wardy rejoined Stacy in front of the house where she sat with her bare feet resting on the dashboard of Olivier's truck. A bottle of pink nail polish was propped in one palm while she deftly painted the nails of her other hand.

Wardy paced the side of the truck. He was fuming. In just a little over an hour, Olivier had succeeded in getting more come-hither attention from Toni than he ever got in all the years that they had known each other. She was blinded to his hustle – by his *generosity*. On top of that, even his best friend was hanging all over the guy. Fred seemed oblivious to Olivier's hostile attitude toward him. He seemed to think the guy was great – fawned all over him almost as much as Toni did.

He flat out didn't like the guy and he told himself that Toni's interest in him had nothing to do with it.

He could not exactly put his finger on what it was about Olivier that he found odd, but as far as he was concerned there was something off about the guy. While they were in the garage, he had wasted no time letting Wardy know that he was not welcome. When neither Fred nor Toni were paying attention, Olivier calmly watched him with animosity in his eyes. When he discreetly cocked his head toward the door, Wardy took the hint and walked away with his tail tucked between his legs. *At least that's how he felt now.*

As far as he was concerned, the guy was missing a few screws. The sooner they were back on the road the better.

"I gotta pee," Stacy yelled.

***

The barn served as a makeshift garage which Toni explored while listening to Fred and Olivier talk. They stood together in front of an old car that Olivier was restoring.

"It belonged to my father. When he left, I decided to keep it – fix it up," he explained.

"A Benz!" Fred said, smiling and shaking his head. He was elated.

Olivier grinned with pride.

"Damn, do I wish I could be there when you finally get it going. How long you been working on it?" Fred circled the car.

He removed his cap and gave his forehead a scratch before plopping the cap back down on his head and leaning over to look beneath the hood of the car.

While they went back and forth about the restoration, Toni surveyed the tool-lined walls of the barn. Her eyes rested on the serrated blades of a row of saws of varying lengths.

"So how far you guys going?" Olivier asked.

"Well," Fred spoke from beneath the hood. "I'm going home to Texas and Toni's running off to California."

"Is that right?" Olivier grinned at her.

He turned to a nearby workbench and began to rummage through miscellaneous parts. He and Fred resumed their conversation.

Several minutes passed before he turned with a friendly smile. "Got your belt."

When Toni returned to the truck, Wardy was standing several feet from the house oddly staring out toward the garden while Stacy sat in the cluttered bed of the truck with a blank expression on her face. She jumped, snapping from her daydream when Toni climbed in back with her.

"You alright?" she asked.

Stacy nodded, staring forlornly at the back of Wardy's head.

Behind them Fred drove the van around front of the house. "Hey, Wardy! Let's go, man," he called happily from the window.

He stepped from the van with a grinning Olivier and they stood chatting while Wardy made a slow approach. A fine sheen of sweat covered his forehead. He passed them without speaking and climbed into the van. Fred watched him with a curious frown, but Olivier ignored Wardy – continued to speak to Fred as if he didn't exist. Toni wondered at not only Wardy's strange behavior but Stacy's as well.

"I'll follow you guys back to the road to make sure

everything is okay," Olivier was saying.

Toni approached him with an outstretched hand. "Thanks for your help."

He cradled both her hands in his own a little longer than was necessary. They gazed into each other's eyes. "Anytime you're in the area, feel free to stop by." His voice was full of meaning.

"I will," she replied too quickly. Her heart fluttered in her chest.

True to his word, he followed them to the road and trailed them for several miles before honking his horn and turning in the opposite direction to head home.

"Man, were we lucky or what?" Fred removed his cap and tossed it on the dashboard.

Toni nodded her agreement then turned to look into the backseat. *Stacy was too quiet.* She narrowed her eyes at Wardy. "Why you guys acting so weird?"

Wardy and Stacy exchanged troubled glances.

"Guys?" she pushed.

To her surprise, Stacy began to sob uncontrollably.

CHAPTER THREE

Olivier knelt at the foot of the stairs and cradled his mother's limp body in his arms. Her cloudy eyes stared back at him but she was too still. Her features were slack-jawed – her mouth agape. He rocked there on the floor with her. He gasped for air because of the exploding pain in his chest. He enclosed her small hand in his own and brushed his lips across her fingers...

They planned together – he and his mother – to escape Georges and start a brand new life. They were careful – patient for a whole year while Simone pilfered away items that Georges would not miss – money Olivier stole from his pockets after he had fallen into a drunken slumber.

When the day finally came, Olivier lay in bed fully clothed and waited for her. Beneath the sheets near his right hand was a small backpack that carried two sets of clothing including underwear and his toothbrush just as his mother had instructed. And because he would not leave it behind, there was also the small chalkboard that he used to practice his letters.

He was nervous waiting for her. He wondered if she would make it – if she was alright. His father's ranting had ended at least an hour before without any loud crashes or breaking glass and he could no longer hear his mother crying. He knew from experience that by now Georges had more than likely passed out on the couch and he reached for the backpack, reassured by its presence, and hoped as hard as he could that she would come soon.

Outside his bedroom window the sky was a deep, inky black. The moon sat full and round, peering through his window and casting bright yellow light across the floorboards. Had it been any other night, he would have stood at the window and watched for bats. Tonight, he was way too nervous for that. He felt an urgent need to be quiet, as if his life depended on it. As if the slightest step would disturb his father's sleep and send him into a waking rage.

After a time, he dozed, unconsciously pulling the

blanket up around his chin and nestling into the pillow, but suddenly she was there – her smooth, light brown skin was bruised and swollen around her mouth, but her doll-like features were still beautiful. She held a slender finger to her lips. Her dark eyes were round – panicked. Her features tense.

She held a hand out to him and when he placed his hand in her own he found that the soft flesh of her palm was ice cold.

"Come now, Olivier," she whispered.

He gave her hand a squeeze to give her strength while in the other he carried his bag. When they stepped out into the hallway, they both paused at the head of the staircase with Simone motioning for him to remember to walk on the outside edges of the stairs so that they wouldn't creak.

Olivier watched his mother as they went. They had practiced this together many times before, but tonight Simone was shaky, clumsy even and Olivier prepared himself to break her fall.

The last step seemed to her like a barricade while

Olivier thought of it as a halfway point to escape. She was afraid to cross into the light which cast a soft glow from a lamp in the sitting room. She had begun to cry, was fidgeting with the collar of her cloak, her dark head was bent, dejected.

Olivier could hear his father snoring heavily but muffled as if he lay face down.

"Maman!" Olivier whispered, fiercely.

Her head snapped up and she placed an urgent finger to her lips. Her eyes darted to the sitting room doorway and she craned her neck to see, nodding and exhaling a relieved breath when the soles of Georges' boots came into view.

With seemingly renewed strength, she reached for him and he took her hand. Together they stepped from the bottom step causing the wood beneath their feet to give a soft groan and she and Olivier both again paused – stood together holding their breath because Georges' snores quieted to nothing.

But as if they had one mind, they backed away from the stairs together. His small heart pounded in his chest.

Simone was in such a fearful state that her back was covered

in a sheen of sweat while the tender flesh beneath her arms

prickled as if she were being stabbed with dozens of needles.

When the snoring began anew, rising in pitch to its

former level, Olivier and Simone backed away toward the

kitchen, creeping on the tips of their toes, their eyes glued to

Georges' bare back to chart its rise and fall. Their want for the

door, for the freedom of outside air was near strangling and

as they crossed over onto the bright, white linoleum –

linoleum that Simone scrubbed on her hands and knees, she

bumped into the wall with a soft thud before turning with

Olivier and retreating to the back door.

But Georges, who usually collapsed into an

impenetrable drunk stupor, awoke before they could make

their getaway and just as Simone's hand touched the gold,

tarnished doorknob, light flooded the kitchen and Georges

stood in the doorway with a wicked gleam in his eyes. Olivier

rested his head on his mother's hip and cowered behind her.

As Georges crossed the kitchen toward them like a

raging bull, veins popping out in his neck, red eyes bulging,
Simone's shoulders slumped with defeat. She shoved Olivier
away from her and he ran crying to crouch near the
refrigerator with his hands wrapped about his knees. His eyes
moved back and forth between his parents as his father's
anger escalated.

"Please, Georges," Simone pleaded, her hands held out
in front of her.

Georges grabbed her arms – pulled her to him but she
fought his embrace and when he attempted to kiss her, she bit
him.

"You trying to leave me, bitch?" Georges asked while
she struggled. "Where the fuck you think you going?"

And he swung, cocking his arm back and punching
Simone in the chest so hard that she flew into the wall behind
her before crumpling to the floor where she gasped
desperately for air.

"You stupid fucking bitch," Georges screamed, enraged
enough that his breathing was labored.

Still panting for air, Simone pulled herself into a sitting position until she rested against the wall. She struggled to catch her breath, but with her hands pressed to her breast she sneered at Georges. Her eyes brimmed with tears. "I can't stand you, Georges." Her voice conveyed long restrained hatred. "Fucking bastard," she hissed.

An instant of pain crossed Georges face before he fell upon her, grabbing her by the head, twisting her long hair around his fist and dragging her to her feet. While Olivier screamed, like a wildcat Simone fought, kicking and clawing at his face until he drove a knee into her stomach hard enough that her knees buckled. With her curled into a ball on the floor, Georges left her and went to the sink. He angrily snatched open cupboards and threw utensils to the floor.

"You hate me? Okay, bitch," Georges spat while continuing his frantic search. "Okay."

He left the sink with a fork, a threatening piece of silver clasped tightly in his hands, an evil smile on his face.

"Where the fuck did you think you were going?" he

thundered as he approached her.

Simone scrambled to her feet, kicking at Georges when he pounced on her and drug her back down to the linoleum.

"Please, Georges. Please!"

Seemingly in a trance, Georges ignored her screams, overpowered her in her struggles until he had her head securely locked within the crook of his elbow and for moments he held her like that – the two of them kneeling on the floor, Simone's arms and legs flailing uselessly, body jerking as she tried to free herself.

"You're gonna love me, bitch," Georges said.

And Olivier cried out loud almost driven mad by his mother's pain ridden screams. His eyes blurred with tears and his eyes fell to the floor to count the red droplets that pooled beneath her jerking body.

The struggle lasted for mere seconds and ended with Georges shoving Simone away from him and throwing the fork to the floor. He left the house then, slamming the front door behind him. Then came the loud roar of the truck's engine and tires kicking up grass and dirt.

Simone lay on the floor in the fetal position with her sleeve pressed to her face. Her sobbing was pained, defeated. Olivier helped her to her feet and led her to the sink. With her face beneath the faucet, she allowed the water to run over her face until it swirled down the drain, running pure red.

"Simone!"

Olivier froze at the foot of the stairs, almost dropping the handful of items he held – bread, orange juice, and jars of peanut butter and jelly. In his hand he held a butter knife – was careful not to trip lest the knife jab him in the eyeball and he would be blinded the same as his mother. Then he too would have a head wrapped in bulky gauze. Then he too would cry red tears.

"Simone!"

His father had been missing for some time – ever since the bad accident when he'd gotten upset. Days passed without him – with Olivier helping his mother along – him scavenging the kitchen for food. Him cowering in a corner while she

suffered from claustrophobia, suffered terrible bouts of

hysteria because she could not see.

The mornings were the worst where she would sit in

her bedroom perched on the edge of her bed with slumped

shoulders, hair matted and kinky while she cried red tears.

This morning he had tried his best to cheer her – had sung his

letters and when she'd smiled and asked for food, he sprinted

down to the kitchen in search of what she'd asked for.

But now Georges was back.

His father's heavily booted feet crossed the kitchen

floor and then the man appeared in the hall filling the

doorway with his broad frame. His pinstriped suit was

perfectly tailored. His hat was pulled low over his face. With

long strides he passed Olivier, stepping around him as if he

didn't exist.

Olivier stood as tall as his father's thigh – average size

for his six years. He was a beautiful boy - a rich, golden brown

with a head full of short, dark curls, serious dark brown eyes and thick brows. He was a quiet child – solemn yet inquisitive.

His mother said that he was his father's twin. Soft as cotton...

Butterflies did somersaults in his stomach. He watched the booted feet climb the stairs. He listened to his father's heavy breathing and tried to gauge his mood.

"Simone!"

His knees began to tremble. Upstairs, Simone's frightened, soft sobs filled the hallway followed by a door slamming. There was the tell-tale screeching of a dresser being laboriously dragged across the floor to barricade the door. Olivier slowly climbed the stairs, hiding against the rail to watch Georges stand at the bedroom door with his forehead resting against the whitewood.

"Simone," he sung.

In the end, Georges kicked the bedroom door in and Olivier sat on the stairs and cried when the first slap sounded.

"You see this thing, Simone?" Georges growled. "I'll do whatever I want to you. Now give me a kiss."

Simone's screams mingled with the noise of fabric ripping and Olivier pressed his hands to his ears so he wouldn't hear his father's hateful laughter.

Olivier knelt at the foot of the stairs and stroked the salt and pepper hair covering his mother's head. He rocked her dead body in his arms and stared desperately up the stairs searching for answers. *How had she fallen?*

When grief overtook him, he collapsed on the floor beside her. His roar of pain and anger shook the house.

CHAPTER FOUR

Fred stomped on the brakes and the van lurched to a halt.

"Are you kidding me!" he screamed. "You killed somebody?"

Stacy began to wail. "It was an accident," she sobbed, rocking in her seat. "I mean, I think it was an accident. Right, Wardy?"

Wardy turned and nervously stared out the rear window. "We can't just sit here, Fred. We should go."

"No. We gotta turn back," Toni said.

"No way," Wardy protested. "They'll say we killed her."

"We can't just leave like that. He helped us."

"Please, baby," Stacy begged. "It wasn't our fault."

Her voice wavered. To Toni, she didn't sound so sure.

The sun found Olivier leaning against the house holding a fifth of vodka by the neck. He took a long drink from the bottle then swished the bitter liquid around in his mouth before swallowing – oblivious to the hot trail it made down his throat before settling into a warm pool in his stomach. His attention was focused on the yellow, rippling sea of flowers. He had enclosed the immense garden and sat a small gazebo within it because when it rained his mother enjoyed sitting outside in prayer. During the summer, she would retreat into the small field of twisting, yellow blooms in her bare feet while her lips moved in whispered pleas. The flowers had been her favorite – cultivated and pampered for over a decade by his very own hands.

He stood now near the shovel, his hands and clothes covered with soil from uprooting a large patch of the bright flowers. He blocked out the noise of the Rottweiler's endless barking and took another huge swallow of liquor. His eyes moved pass the garden where farther beyond the field sat another enclosed patch of space much smaller than the garden, a 10x10 square of earth fenced in by cheap chicken wire, a small part of the land that he had pitted and used to burn trash in.

How had she fallen? That question nagged at his brain.

She knew the house like the back of her hand – where every piece of furniture sat, the number of paces from her bedroom to the bathroom. And she definitely knew where the stairs were.

His father had made sure of it.

The wire fence leaned to one side threatening to fall over into the pit. The grass surrounding the fence was sunburned, brown and bald in some spots, untended and neglected when compared with the rest of the land.

His eyes fell thoughtfully to the ground where Simone lay wrapped in a blanket before again resting on the trash pit – a space suited for its purpose.

"Maman! Maman, dites l'alphabet!"

Olivier skipped in circles around his mother who sat still and cross-legged on the floor. It was the time of day where she showed him his letters – where she pulled out the small chalkboard and together they would sing and make words with blue or red chalk. Her favorite color was red and his was blue. But today she seemed sad and Olivier wanted to cheer her up. He knew that his mother liked for him to sing the alphabet or say his numbers, but when he started their favorite tune, she didn't sing along with him so he stopped in front of her and wondered if her face hurt and if maybe that was the reason why she wouldn't sing.

Then he remembered the letter from grandma.

Sometimes when they were alone together in the house, his mother would take out her letter from grandma and read it. Now that she couldn't see, she could no longer read the letter that admonished her to "stick with Georges" because he was a "good man who provided well for her; that she was lucky to have him".

Each time she read it, his mother would cry. "Mother, he buried me in the yard. He buried me in the back yard for hours."

Olivier nodded – a silent witness – reluctantly recalling all the bad things that Georges did to his mother. He had been there.

He was always there. But now she was so different.

"Maman?" he queried.

When her head bowed, her shoulders began to quake and he sunk to his knees before her, crawling into her lap and burrowing against her. She wrapped her arms around him - held him to her as sobs wracked her body.

"I love you, Maman," he whispered.

Even after her sobs subsided she rocked him in her arms. Olivier's eyes remained fixed on the gauze that he helped her wrap each day around her head like a blindfold.

When his father finally called her from the kitchen, he knew the words that would come from her mouth before she spoke them. He knew that he could not protect her. She whispered to him, her voice thick with fear...

"Run, Olivier."

Once Simone was gently deposited into her grave in the midst of the sunflower field, Olivier calmly strode to the shed with the shovel in his hand. When the wooden door swung open and the large black dog leapt from the dark growling, canines bared but stunted by the chain around its neck, Olivier swung the shovel like a baseball bat, face fixed in an angry snarl, satisfied at the noise of metal striking bone and the dog's yelp of pained surprise. The large animal flew back into the shed and skidded across the floor to rest in an unconscious heap.

***

Olivier let his head fall back to allow the shower's warm spray to wash away his tears. The shower ran cold before he was all cried out and he stepped from the tub and mechanically ran a bath towel over his body. His muscles were tired, sore from stress and exertion. His insides were near numb – his mind dull.

He had failed to protect her. Again.

He stumbled naked from the bathroom meaning to

go in search of his vodka bottle. As he started across the hall toward the stairs a shiny, colorful object caught his eye. In his grief he almost ignored it, but curiosity caused him to lean over and pick up the tightly folded piece of cellophane. His heart thudded in his chest. He opened the gum wrapper then slid the small square of wax paper away and brought it to his nose.

It still carried the sweet scent of cherry bubblegum.

CHAPTER FIVE

Everyone was quiet save for Stacy who could be heard crying quietly from the backseat. Wardy sat across from her nervously tapping his sneakered foot on the worn rug. Toni sat up front with Fred biting her nails. Though she wasn't cold, she was shivering. A lump of guilt and fear rested in her stomach. Fred adjusted then re-adjusted the rear view mirror as an excuse to check the road they left behind.

Tony said what they all needed to hear. "I got a bad feeling about this. We should go to the police."

"No, no." Stacy sobbed. "We can't."

"We can." Toni turned in her seat. "Right now it looks like we're running."

"Running from what?" Wardy snapped. "Who's to say that we were in the house? Geez. I wish you would just shut up about it already."

Toni turned back around in her seat and shook her head. Tears burned the back of her eyes. She hoped that

Olivier was alright.

Stacy spoke quietly from the backseat. "You couldn't reach her?" She stared at Wardy but grabbed her chest as if in pain.

"I tried." Wardy's tone was flat. "I couldn't make it to her before she fell."

"You guys should've said something back at the house," Fred said, his voice grieved. "The guy tried to help us." Fred startled them all by slamming his fist against the dashboard. "This is so fucked up! Why did you just walk into the guy's house?"

"Stop cursing at me!" Stacy screamed hysterically. "I had to use the fucking bathroom!"

Toni jumped as Fred's fist this time made contact with the steering wheel. His plump, dark face was screwed up into a scowl. Several seconds passed in silence.

"I didn't touch her. No way I'm going down for that," Wardy said.

"Yeah?" Fred glared at him through the rearview

mirror. "You know how cold-blooded this shit is? I mean, I wish you two wouldn't have made the choice for me. I don't want anything to do with this."

"Fred -" Stacy started.

"Just shut up, Stacy."

"Let's just go back to Olivier and explain what happened." Toni felt terrible.

"No," Wardy said.

"What do you mean no?"

"For all we know, he probably thinks she fell."

"Wow," Toni folded her arms and turned to Fred. "This isn't right."

"Shit," Fred cursed.

"Fred, are you really gonna sit here and let this bitch convince you to turn your girl in?" Wardy exclaimed.

"What the fuck, Wardy!" Fred again slammed his hand down on the steering wheel and the van swerved on the road. "We wouldn't be in this shit if you two had stayed by the truck."

"Just drop me off at the nearest rest stop."

Not wanting Wardy to get away so quickly, Toni pointed to a passing sign. "There's a diner at the next exit. Let's just pull over there. We can sit and clear our heads."

Wardy sighed. "Just drop me –"

"Shut up, Wardy," Fred said.

He pulled off at the next exit and drove in silence to the small roadside diner. Toni was the first to get out. She planned to drink a cup of coffee while persuading Fred to drive to the nearest police station. Inside the nearly empty diner they all sat together in a booth without speaking. After their coffee was served, Toni spoke up.

"Maybe we should call him."

Wardy's eyes were on fire with suspicion. "Why?" he asked.

"I don't know," she shrugged. "Just to help us decide what we should do next."

He rested his elbows on the table and leaned toward her. "So I guess that means you have his number?"

Toni returned his glare but didn't speak.

"I have his number." Fred stood and reached into his pocket.

Wardy frowned at him. "You give him your number too?"

"Yeah." Fred nodded. "We exchanged numbers just in case I was ever in the area. You know, normal shit that people do when they're not throwing old ladies down stairs."

"She wasn't that old," Stacy whispered. Her eyes were swollen and rimmed red from crying.

Without speaking, Fred turned and exited the restaurant. As he approached the outside phone booth, Wardy ran an anxious hand over his face. While Stacy sat biting her nails, Toni got up from the booth and followed Fred outside.

The paint on the kitchen cabinets had yellowed with age as had the walls. Light played off the dusty ceiling, turning cobwebs into dark shadows that inhabited the corners.

Olivier sat stark naked at the kitchen table and inhaled the sugary scent from the thin, rainbow colored cellophane wrapper. He doubted that it had been purposely discarded – thought it was more than likely lost – but to him, the mystery was solved. He recalled that the girl...Stacy...had offered him gum while popping her own loudly between her teeth. Between her fingers, she rolled the colorful cellophane before folding it and tucking the wrapper into the pocket of her jeans.

His first impulse had been to jump into his truck and tear down Route 10 in search of them but they were long gone. It would be what his father called a "dummy mission."

But what he did have was Fred's address in Dallas and he planned to leave for Texas as soon as possible. Fred promised to call on him when he drove Stacy back home to Shreveport, but he doubted that would happen now. And Olivier didn't want to run the risk of reaching Fred after the four of them split up. He wanted them all together.

They had used him. His fist clenched and unclenched on the table. His breathing became ragged. The shrill ringing of the telephone startled him.

It hardly ever rang and he had forgotten about it. His mother sometimes used it to call his grandmother, but that was rare. He barely touched the phone at all.

Now he sat with it gripped tightly in one hand but pressed firmly to his ear.

Fred sounded as if he hadn't expected an answer. "Hello, Olivier? It's Fred."

"Hey, Fred," Olivier said. He was so shocked to hear Fred's voice that he almost fell over in his chair. He took a deep breath and attempted to steady the tremor in his own tone.

"Olivier..." Fred started but his voice trailed off.

"Hey, Fred. Listen, man. I'm glad you called. I've had an accident here. I'm in a little trouble and I could use some help."

"Oh, yeah?" Fred released a weary sigh. "What's going on?"

"Well, you know I'm stuck here almost in the middle of nowhere. I hate to bother you, but my mother fell down the stairs. She's hurt pretty bad."

Silence.

"She says that someone was in the house. That she heard a young girl laughing."

The silence was replaced with heavy breathing.

"It's nothing to worry about. It's just that I have to pass your address over to the cops. They're asking questions." Olivier paused. "I'm not blaming you guys or anything but you know..."

"Yeah, about that...listen, man," Fred's tone distant. "I didn't know about that until we got down the road. Stacy and Wardy were afraid to say anything."

Olivier balled his fist on the table. His voice was strained. "Did they say what happened?"

Again silence followed and Olivier bit his tongue to

stop himself from screaming.

"And you say she's alright, eh?" Fred asked after several moments passed.

Olivier gritted his teeth. *After all he had done for them and the guy was playing dumb.*

"Yeah, yeah," Olivier replied, twisting the cellophane wrapper between his fingers. "But see the thing is that the cops – they wanna talk to you guys, you know, just to fill in any blanks. You think you could turn around? Or I could just pass your address along to them so they can track you down in Dallas."

"We gotta go back," Fred said slamming the phone down and heading toward the van.

Stacy began to cry again.

"What did he say?" Wardy asked warily.

"She's alive." Fred actually sounded relieved. He turned the key in the ignition.

"What?" Stacy gasped. "How?"

"I don't know," Fred answered with a smile on his face. "I guess she was just hurt. The police want to talk to us though." He turned in his seat with narrowed eyes. His voice was stern. "And we're gonna turn around and handle this like we should've done in the first place. It really looks bad that we just took off like that." Fred turned and shook his head in disappointment. As the van rolled out of the parking lot and headed back to the highway he chastised Wardy and Stacy. "I can't believe you guys didn't check to see if she was breathing."

Stacy ignored Fred. "She's alive!" she screamed at the top of her lungs. She leapt toward the front seat and grabbed Toni in a hug. A broad grin spread across her pretty face.

In the back seat, Wardy remained quiet.

They left the sun-filled sky behind them and turned onto the shaded, dusky road. Stacy sat humming softly to herself while Toni sat up front and nervously worried her bottom lip with her teeth. Fred squinted at the road as he drove. He was tired and agitated and the anticipation of dealing with Olivier and the police weighed heavily on his mind. He stared into the rear view mirror and peered at Wardy. He was concerned about what Wardy would say. Not even an hour had passed since he'd last asked Fred to drop him by the side of the road.

"It looks bad that we left," Toni whispered.

"Why don't you shut your big mouth." Wardy's tone was low, menacing. "Goody-two-shoe ass."

"Just tell the truth and everything will be fine," Fred said.

"Shut up, Wardy," Toni said, agitated.

"If it wasn't for you smiling in his damn face –"

"Nobody told your dumb ass to go in his house," Toni screamed, turning in her seat. "Stupid mother –"

"I wish both of y'all would shut the hell up!" Fred shouted, slamming his hand down on the steering wheel.

The van swerved, threatening to go off the road and

into the trees. Toni and Wardy continued to glare at one another and Stacy started to cry.

"It was our fault. We scared her," she sobbed.

"It's alright, baby," Fred said. "It's alright. Just tell'em what happened. It'll be fine."

Inside the van was thick with tension.

"This shit ain't right, Fred. I'm telling you that woman was dead," Wardy said.

"But how do you know? You didn't check her. You telling me this man lying about his mama?"

"I'm saying this shit don't feel right."

"It don't feel right?" Fred said, suddenly outraged. The van again swerved on the road. "You watch somebody mama fall down some stairs – a person that helped you – then you run off like nothing happened? That's some bullshit, Wardy. You trying to save your own ass. That's what you doing."

Wardy kicked Fred's seat. "Why'd you leave us? You know Stacy can't sit still." He shook his head and chuckled to himself. "You and this goofy ass bitch right here got a whole lot of nerve."

"Screw you, Wardy," Toni retorted.

He ignored her. "Why you ain't turn around in the first place, Fred? Tell me that."

"Whatever, man."

"'Cause you ain't want your girl to get locked up?" Wardy's voice was sing-song. He sat back in his seat. "Better get your shit together, Freddie baby. We all in this one together. I'm telling you – there's some shit in the game."

They rode the last few miles to Olivier's in silence and when they turned down the lane leading to his property, Toni exhaled a pent up, pained breath. Once they reached the land surrounding Olivier's house Wardy moved forward between them and stared out the windshield.

"There's two cars parked out front. You see'em?" he said, pointing.

Toni chewed at the stubby nail of her thumb. "Must be the cops."

"Yeah," he replied, brow furrowed. "But I don't see Olivier's truck."

"Might be around back," Fred said.

He slowed as they approached the house, coming to halt beside two dusty Fords. In spite of the brightness of day, they could see lights that were on inside the house. They heard Olivier call out to them as they exited the van.

"Hey, guys. We're back here." He waved for them to come around back.

Toni wrapped a reassuring arm around her cousin's waist and Stacy gave her a grateful smile.

"Around back?" Wardy whispered harshly. "Really?"

"Shut up, Wardy," Fred spoke over his shoulder. As they walked along the side of the house, he quickened his pace.

Wardy dejectedly stuffed his hands into his pockets.

Toni rubbed a reassuring hand along Stacy's back while glaring behind her at Wardy. She was glad that Fred had returned in spite of Wardy's protest. She took a deep breath and prepared herself to talk to the police – to be there to support her once happy-go-lucky cousin whose head now sat lowered with shame and worry.

They both jumped as the shed erupted with an insistent, vicious barking. Claws scratched violently at the flimsy door and wood splintered as the large animal pounded against it. In fear, she paused and held Stacy against her, petrified at the thought of a huge, snarling dog bursting from the shed and charging them with bared canines.

"Oh, shit," Wardy exclaimed.

Over the barking came another sound – a sickening thud – and they turned from a fleeing Wardy in just enough time to catch the end swing – the long, muscular length of Olivier's arms perfectly extended, the end of a steel bat reaching out to catch an arc of blood as it leapt from Fred's skull before his round body fell to the ground in a heap then the terrible sight of Olivier falling upon him and spending his rage.

"Run!"

Toni turned to see Wardy fleeing on swift legs toward the trees.

Olivier disappeared, leaving Fred's quivering, dead body on the ground. When he reappeared with a rifle, he first charged them like a wild, rabid animal. Stacy flew from her arms as a blow from Olivier's heavy fist caught her full in the face, lifting her into the air and knocking one of her shoes off. Toni screamed, flinching as warm blood sprayed her face and Olivier stood over Stacy, stilling her struggles by digging the sole of his boot into her neck. While he aimed at Wardy's retreating back, she choked beneath him.

Crack!

The gun shot rattled the windows of the house. Wardy slipped, momentarily falling to the ground before again jumping to his feet. Olivier took aim then cursed when he found that he didn't have a shot and took off after Wardy toward the thick blanket of trees.

The barking lowered to a threatening growl.

Toni was so afraid that her teeth chattered and she watched the trees while trying to shake Stacy into consciousness.

"Stacy," she said, looking around for Olivier.

The shed was silent.

"Stacy, please," she whispered frantically. She drug Stacy into a sitting position. She grabbed her by the chin and smacked her face.

What if he watched them right now from the trees?

Stacy jolted awake, kicking at Toni and moving to cower against the house. "Where is he?" she sputtered. Her face had begun to swell.

"He's looking for Wardy." Toni's eyes strayed to Fred. She took a deep breath and started to move toward him but Stacy snatched her back.

"Don't go," she pleaded, her eyes round with terror.

"I have to get the keys," Toni whispered fiercely, loosening Stacy's grip on her sweater.

When she neared him she fell to her knees, terrified

and heartbroken at the sight of his battered body and she sobbed while searching his pockets. She avoided looking at his face. Her heart trembled because of the blood covering her hands.

Crack!

She ducked and on instinct fell flat to the ground as birds squawked and took to the sky in a loud flapping of startled wings. Fred's body was still warm where it pressed into her side. The grass was dry and cool beneath her palms.

Go, Toni. She was dizzy. Her heart beat painfully against the ground. She was too afraid to move.

Crack! Crack!

Tears burned her eyes. Behind her, Stacy screamed.

Was Wardy dead? Somewhere laying in the dirt with his head blown off?

If he was, then Olivier was on his way back to the house.

I don't wanna die.

Toni turned again to search Fred's pockets. When she

had the keys, she ran back to Stacy on shaky legs. She helped her to her feet and half-carried her alongside the house and back to the van. Through blinding tears she pushed Stacy through the driver's side door and then crawled in after her. Her hands shook uncontrollably and she paused and forced herself to take a deep breath. Even after she found the right key, it took several seconds before her trembling hands could make it fit into the ignition. When the engine turned over, she threw the van into drive and tore away from the house.

Paranoia screamed that Olivier would be standing nearby with a gun aimed at the moving van, a sinister smile plastered on his handsome face – and she was afraid to look anywhere but straight ahead. She reminded herself that if they didn't make it they would die – that Olivier surely meant to murder them just as he had Fred.

The fine hairs on the back of her neck stood on end. It wasn't far until they hit Route 10 and she held her breath and picked up speed, anxious to put as much distance as she could between them and Olivier's house. The tires kicked up clumps of dirt and the van bounced hard over the uneven terrain. She gripped the steering wheel as hard as she could, the sound of her heartbeat thundering in her ears, her eyes intent on the road before her.

By the time she saw the large, red truck it was too late. It appeared seemingly from nowhere headed straight for the van. Just before they were t-boned, Toni saw Olivier leap from the truck, rolling in a somersault while the pickup barreled toward them.

There was the loud crashing of metal impacting metal and Stacy's slender body sailing through the air then the loud shattering of glass when she flew through the windshield. She landed on the hood of the truck, twisted and gasping for her last breath. A large shard of glass protruded from her neck. The van toppled on its side and slid fast toward the trees before wrapping around a red oak – nothing more than a bent hunk of metal.

Inside, Toni lay in the fetal position on the broken

glass of the exploded passenger window. The metallic taste of blood in her mouth sent her into an uncontrollable bout of coughing and she choked – struggled for air. The loud whir of tires spinning and Olivier's humming were the only sounds she could hear. She fought unconsciousness – blinked warm blood from her eyes. Olivier's booted feet came into view and he grunted before Stacy's lifeless body fell to the ground in front of her, blank eyes fixed on her face.

If she could make it into the trees, she might have a chance of getting away…

"Toni."

Olivier fell to his knees and smiled at her through the broken windshield.

"Olivier, please," She begged.

"Olivier, please," he mimicked. His eyes were blocks of ice.

He crawled into the van and Toni flinched at the sight of the rifle. His breath was hot on her face. He laid the muzzle against her eye and Toni winced at the feel of the cold steel pressed into her skin.

When he pulled the trigger, Toni screamed – expected a flash of penetrating, searing light then imminent darkness but there was nothing but a hard click and Olivier's cruel laughter. An uncontrollable shiver dominated her body.

Olivier brought the butt of the rifle down into her skull.

CHAPTER SIX

"Just leave me alone, Eugene," Stella said, her voice husky with frustration. She walked to the liquor cabinet and pulled a bottle of cognac from the shelf.

"Don't worry. I'll find her."

Stella took a deep breath to calm her tongue. "Find her where, Eugene? That little bitch is long gone."

"Now hey now –" Eugene started.

"Hey now what?" Stella asked, losing her temper. She slammed her glass down on the table.

With her hands on her hips, she began to pace the floor. The crush velvet of her robe flowed in angry waves with every step.

"Come on, Stella. I'm tired. I'll deal with it tomorrow."

"Yeah? Well, while you're at it you can stop at the bank and get me some more money."

"I told you I'll find her."

Stella wanted to scream. She felt like she was at her breaking point. "Eugene, that heifer ain't took five grand and ran off to New Orleans for the weekend. She gone! Do you understand that? The money is gone." Stella took a step toward Eugene and bent at the waist so that they were eye level, but Eugene averted his gaze so Stella smacked her lips with disgust.

"I don't know what we gone do," he said finally and reclined in his seat.

"What you talking about, Eugene? You told Delphine –"

"I know what I said. Just back off, woman. Okay."

Stella's hands balled into fists at her sides. "What you gone do, Eugene? Huh? When we got married, you promised me that you were gonna –"

Eugene looked defeated. "Ain't no more money, Stella."

"Don't pull that shit with me right now," she warned, wagging a finger at him. "Delphine is counting on you."

"Take it out of your account," Eugene coerced, his gaze softening.

"No!" Stella screamed, hysterical.

"What the hell do you mean no?"

Stella again began to pace the floor. Her hazel eyes blazed with anger. "I'm not paying for it."

Eugene shook his head in disbelief. Under his breath, he gave a low whistle. His words were slightly slurred and he pointed an accusing finger at her. "You one ole selfish ass female." He stumped a foot to emphasize each word and shook his head as if he were ashamed of her.

"No, you're the selfish one. All that gambling and drinking you do is the reason –"

"Naw," Eugene tucked his thumbs into his belt. "That's all that shopping you and Delphine been doing. And let's not forget all that money you've been spending carousing with that Johnson boy."

Stella could not help herself from throwing her head back and laughing. "Well, let's not point no fingers," she said with meaning.

Eugene gave her an assenting smile and nodded.

"Come on, honey. Just for a little while, okay? I'll get it back to you."

Stella tried to bite her tongue to keep from retorting but failed. "You sorry mother –"

"Everything you got I gave you," Eugene interrupted, his face turned up into a drunken sneer. He jabbed a thumb into his chest. "You ain't have shit when I brought you here. Ole dusty ass."

Stella felt as if he had just spit on her and she turned her back to him before she said something that Eugene would regret. She balled her hands into fists until her nails dug into the soft flesh of her palms. In her struggle to control her temper, her breathing came in short spurts. She cursed under her breath. She knew that in the end she would give Delphine the money if for nothing else but to solidify her own future.

"So I expect you to do this," Eugene pushed. "Just until I figure out what happened to, Toni. Okay, baby?"

~***~

Like clockwork, she appeared. Her brown skin seemed to glow as she made it across the field. When her beautiful face came into view, he smiled a deep, secretive grin that creased his face. He knew that she would follow him into the quaint, brick cottage where they frequently met in secret.

Inside he pulled his shirt over his head and revealed a stomach and arms hard and glistening with sweat. When she entered, he was already standing beside the bed removing his pants. The door closed behind her with a loud thump before she moved sensually toward him while pulling a thin, cotton camisole dress over her head.

He admired her small, firm breasts. A dark mole lay to the left of her belly button. His eyes remained on the dark triangle of hair at the apex of her thighs and his mouth watered. When she was close enough to touch, he deeply inhaled her sweet scent, groaning when she reached out and wrapped a soft, warm hand around the base of his manhood.

She pushed him to the bed and knelt in front of him

and his head fell back, a deep, pulsating groan tearing through him when her moist mouth closed around him.

He pulled her to him until the soft, hot flesh of her belly pressed into him. She moaned, throaty and seductive, when he pressed a kiss to her full lips and he tightened his embrace when she rotated her hips against him.

He closed his eyes and reached out to grasp a greedy handful of supple flesh, turning her onto her back and parting her thighs with a knee. She held on to him, kneading the muscles of his back while he moved inside her. Her long legs wrapped about his waist and she bucked her hips wildly beneath him. He cupped her buttocks as a frenzied orgasm tore through her and she melted into him. After it was over, he slowly caressed her back and whispered into her hair while she dozed.

"We have to tell her soon," she said sleepily. "She's gonna be so damn mad."

His eyebrows rose and fell with disregard. They would be married soon. "Just a little while longer, baby."

He smoothed her hair back and brushed a kiss across her temple. As she snored, he held her to him, relishing her while rubbing a lazy hand over her smooth thighs.

CHAPTER SEVEN

Toni awoke face down with a mouthful of sawdust and a pounding headache. She came to with a jolt. Her body instantly clenched, panicked as the day's events came back in a rush. She was afraid to open her eyes – afraid to move at all for fear that Olivier was waiting nearby. Her breathing came in short spurts and when she accidentally inhaled wood particles, she held her breath in an effort to fight back a sneeze.

Somewhere nearby an echoing grinding could be heard combined with a mysterious drumming. To her, it sounded like a tractor, but she couldn't recall seeing one anywhere nearby. Slowly, she opened her eyes and realized that she was in the barn. Her hands were tied behind her back and she grunted at the pain in her arms. The doors were slightly ajar and she could see outside enough to know that it was dusk and that the sun was nowhere to be found. Wardy sat behind her.

"Where's the sheriff?" he asked.

At times her eyes would go out of focus and Toni feared that she would pass out. Wardy, on the other hand was alert and on guard. His feet were roped to the legs of a chair and his arms were tied behind his back. He struggled with the restraints despite the fact that Olivier stood over him.

"What sheriff?" Olivier, surprised at Wardy's question, stared at him with a raised brow.

"The police, damnit! You told Fred that the cops –"

"You really are that stupid."

To Toni, Wardy seemed dazed as well – almost shell shocked even. He shook his head as if to clear his brain but continued to glare at Olivier. His short hair was matted and broken blades of greenish-brown grass clung to his face and clothes.

"The cars parked out front –"

"Just some old junk cars," Olivier explained in a mocking tone. "I never thought you guys would come back. Not in a million years."

Olivier pulled a chair to the middle of the floor and sat. When he was comfortable, he stared at them.

"We're gonna talk." He concentrated on Wardy. "If you decide that you don't want to talk," he turned and pointed out the back of the open barn where just beyond the barn light ended and the dark of night prevailed. In the shadows, a lone machine stood nearby.

"What is that?" Wardy said, glaring hatefully back at him.

"Woodchipper," Toni whispered.

"Man, this some bullshit!" Wardy screamed. "Let me outta here."

Olivier was stone faced. "What happened to my mother, Wardy?"

Toni started to cry.

"How about you?" he asked her.

"You killed Fred," she sobbed.

"Yeah." His eyes searched her face. "Fred was a nice guy, wasn't he?"

Toni shivered and her teeth chattered causing a distinct clicking noise though it was extremely warm in the barn. Mosquitos played around their heads and Toni rubbed her cheek across her shoulder to rid herself of one of the annoying insects. Her face was wet with tears.

"You didn't have to kill him."

"Humph." Olivier turned to face Wardy. "Why were you in my house?" He held a hand up when Wardy opened his mouth to speak. "Don't lie," Olivier said, reaching in his pocket and finding the colored cellophane. "Don't you lie."

"Where's your mother?" Toni asked. By the way that Olivier watched Wardy, she knew it was only a matter of time before he ended up just like Fred and Stacy. She didn't want to be alone with him. *She wasn't ready yet.*

"I don't have a mother anymore." Olivier spoke calmly, matter-of-factly. It seemed to Toni like he was two people – one affable and kind, the other malicious and cruel.

"Lied about that too, eh?" Wardy's tone was self-righteous.

Will you shut up..."Are you going to kill us, Olivier?" she asked from her place on the ground.

His eyes remained on Wardy. "I helped you all. Helped you. And you wouldn't even show me common human decency as your fellow man." His voice broke. He leaned forward and rested his elbows on his knees. "Look how you repaid me."

Toni could not help but feel sorry for him. He was right. "Olivier –"

"Don't talk to his crazy ass," Wardy interrupted.

Olivier expelled a labored breath and sat back in his seat. He looked exhausted. His tone was once again friendly but deadly serious. "So things are gonna go like this – Wardy, I'm gonna take a bat and beat your head in if you don't tell me what happened."

No, no. "It was an accident," Toni cried out. "Tell him, Wardy."

"Then spit it out!" Olivier screamed. His face contorted into the violent visage of the Olivier from the road.

Wardy was resigned to his fate. "He gone kill us anyway. You think he really gonna let us walk outta here to bring the police right back to his crazy ass?"

"Tell me what happened."

Toni and Wardy stared at one another for several seconds, him shaking his head and her biting her lip. Olivier waited patiently.

"Stacy had to pee," he started.

"So you went to the house?" Olivier prompted.

He nodded.

Olivier's eyes were intent on his face. "Then what happened?"

Wardy's eyes rested on Toni. "Promise me you'll let her go."

Olivier turned and looked over his shoulder at her. He nodded. "Okay. You have my word."

Wardy stared at his feet. "We were out by the truck. Like I said, she had to use the bathroom..."

~***~

"You can hold it, Stace." Wardy was agitated. "We'll be back on the road in no time. First service station bathroom is yours."

Stacy pushed open the rusty door and jumped down from the truck. "What's wrong, dear. You mad 'cause Toni and that gorgeous, muscle ridden stud are making eyes at one another?"

"Shut up, Stacy."

She giggled. "You don't like him, do you?"

"Shit no." Wardy turned to look over his shoulder.

Stacy slammed the rusted door closed behind her. She stretched, raising slender arms above her head and giving a small grunt while staring up at the house. "I wonder if anyone is home."

"Why don't you just wait until he comes back?"

"Why when I can just knock on the door? I doubt he lives all the way out here by himself. Besides," Stacy said, "aren't you curious about him?"

"I think something is wrong with him." Wardy held two fingers out at her as if issuing a hex.

Stacy rolled her eyes and stared up at the three story structure. "He sure has a nice house."

Wardy sighed stuffing his hands into the pockets of his jeans. *This guy...*

"Let's knock." Stacy said, bounding up the stairs two at a time.

Wardy did not climb the porch but waited while Stacy rapped loudly on the door.

"Hello!"

She peered into windows draped with flowing lace curtains. "Someone's playing music inside."

"Wait," Wardy said when she pressed her ear to the door.

But against his protest, Stacy reached out and turned the knob, pushing the white wooden door inward.

"You can't just invite yourself into someone's house, Stace," he complained.

Stacy stood just within the threshold and peered into the darkened hall. Up ahead lay a staircase but otherwise the interior of the house was dusky and smelled of flowers. She stepped inside, turning her head to look behind her as Wardy joined her near the door. Soft music drifted down the stairs.

"Hello!" Stacy yelled.

"Shhhh!" Wardy turned on her with a frown and pressed a finger to his lips.

Again Stacy rolled her eyes and left him standing at the door. To their left sat a dim kitchen where the hum of the refrigerator mingled with the steady ticking of a clock from the sitting room to their right. While music played overhead, Stacy stepped into the shadowy room, hesitant because the drapes were drawn and gave the high back chairs the appearance of being occupied by shadows.

The furniture was old-fashioned – outdated even – the couch and chairs a faded blue and covered with plastic. The hardwood floor had been polished to a high gloss shine that matched the wood paneled walls. On the floor beneath the coffee table lay an old threadbare rug. On the mantel all by itself sat a large, silver picture frame that held a photo bearing the resemblance of a young Olivier and an older man and woman who Stacy assumed were his parents. Only the man smiled.

Wardy stood in the doorway and stared around the room while Stacy fingered the white lace doilies on the end tables.

"Why do you think he left the music playing?" Wardy asked.

She shrugged and picked up a lone knick-knack – a small, glass unicorn. "Beats me."

"I thought you had to use the bathroom."

"Calm down." Stacy sashayed past him and into the hall where she ventured a careless glance into the kitchen. "The interior would be peachy if someone cared enough to fix it up." She started up the stairs. Her hands lightly trailed the solid oak banister.

Wardy stood at the foot of the stairs. His voice rose over the soft music playing overhead. "You walking through here like you own the place."

Stacy smacked her lips at his sarcastic tone but did not turn to look at him. She could feel him climbing the stairs behind her. The second floor opened into a short hall. Before them was a window covered in the same lace curtains as downstairs. There was another airy, lingering smell of sweetness that Stacy couldn't place. The soft music became more distinct.

Wardy leaned against the wall while Stacy walked to a door and boldly pushed it open to reveal a surprisingly plain bedroom with a neatly made bed. A pair of men's slippers were placed by the door.

The second bedroom revealed the source of music coming from an old phonograph in a bedroom that seemed to belong to a woman. The scent of sweetness was stronger there – almost overwhelming. Unable to help herself, Stacy stepped into the room and threw open the closet doors. She donned a black hat, adjusting it so that the wide flimsy brim fell over one eye. She stepped out of the closet and ran to a vanity. While staring into the mirror she winked and flirtatiously puckered her lips.

She barely noticed when the record stopped.

"Olivier? Is that you, mon bebe?"

Stacy froze.

"Olivier?"

She placed the hat on the bed and crept to the bedroom door on the tips of her toes. She peered around the door and saw a woman standing in the middle of the hallway. Her head was tilted to one side. Her hair was wild and touched by gray. Her skin was smooth and light brown. The gown she wore was faded and thin.

Wardy hid behind the curtains. He stared at the woman with a strange expression on his face. To Stacy he pointed at his eyes. She nodded in understanding. Wardy held a finger to his lips then gestured toward the stairs. Again she nodded and took a hesitant step forward.

"Olivier?" The woman's brow furrowed with confusion and she nervously fingered the hem of her gown.

Wardy stepped out from behind the curtains with his arms out at his side and attempted to move around the woman. Stacy made her way toward the stairs.

"Who's there?"

Together they froze. Their eyes met and held.

The woman backed away, blocking Stacy's path. She cursed. There was no way she would make it around the woman without being detected. Wardy took a cautious step forward and a floorboard groaned beneath his feet.

"Who's there, damnit?"

Go! Wardy urgently mouthed the word to her.

Just as Stacy and Wardy started to maneuver around her, she took a cautious step backward. Stacy attempted to rush past her and in the process bumped into her. The woman yelled in surprise and stumbled backward. Stacy screamed and rushed toward her with outstretched arms, alarmed when the woman tumbled headfirst down the stairs. Her fingers barely touched the hem of the woman's gown but she ran behind her – face screwed up in angst because she knew that she would be unable to catch the woman who flew down the stairs without touching a step only to land sprawled on the wooden floor below. Her twisted head faced the door.

"And that's what happened?" Olivier asked seeming convinced.

"I swear," Wardy replied.

"Why didn't you say something to her?" He rose to his feet and walked across the barn. "Ask to use the toilet? She would've understood."

Wardy didn't reply.

Olivier returned with the pitchfork. He held the tines over Wardy's lap pressed into his genitals.

"Simone!" Georges voice was filled with panic.

"Son of a bitch."

"Maman..." Olivier stood in the doorway of the bathroom and pleaded with his mother.

He was in his room when her screaming started. He had been so engrossed in his airplane model that he didn't hear his father enter the house. His thoughts had also been on Joslyn Daniels, the prettiest girl in the ninth grade.

While he made his way down the hallway toward the bathroom, he did so with a frown on his face. He pushed his sleeves up as he went and readied himself to box his father for terrorizing his mother, but when he rounded the doorway, his heart dropped into his stomach.

A lone candle burned on a nearby table – a candle that Olivier insisted stay in the bathroom when his mother bathed. The glow of light revealed a naked Simone sitting on the floor. Her wet hair was plastered to her face. In front of her, a begging Georges was on his knees. His eyes were wide and bloodshot. Simone held a shotgun pressed into his throat.

Her gaze was blank but in the glow of candlelight her eyes seemed a terrible black. Her face was contorted with *hatred. She lay on the floor in a puddle of water. Her legs were wrapped around Georges' waist.*

"Maman," Olivier whispered soothingly.

"Get out, Olivier," she screamed, her voice cracking with bloodlust.

Olivier's eyes remained on the gun – his father's gun. A gun that had forever sat on a closet shelf in their bedroom.

How had she gotten it? How had she loaded it?

"Maman, please," Olivier cried, his hands pressed together as if in prayer.

Simone turned her head, her eyes moving as if searching for him. Georges cried out because he knew his fate was sealed.

Olivier held his breath when their eyes met. She smiled.

"Maman..."

"I'm sorry, Olivier," she whispered.

"Maman, no!"

Olivier fell to his knees, startled by the loud blast from the shotgun, overtaken by dizziness and a ringing in his ears, overwhelmed with horror at the sight of his father's head

exploding and the sight forever burned to memory of the

triumph – the expression of joyous satisfaction on his mother's

face as Georges' blood washed over her naked body in streams

– forceful jets of realized revenge and she gave a deep

gratified sigh.

They sat there together for several minutes with

Simone lying eerily still, seemingly a corpse just as bloody as

Georges covered in a ghostlike glow from the candlelight

flickering over her.

Without speaking, Olivier rose and went to her. She

relinquished the gun and he set it aside then lifted her from

the floor. Once again that night, he laid her inside the now

cooling tub of water. This time he washed blood from her

body. Simone sat still with a peaceful expression on her face

and allowed him to carry her to her bedroom where he dried

her and pulled a gown over her head. Olivier tucked her into

bed and pulled the blankets up to her chin before smoothing

her hair back and placing a kiss on her forehead. He left her there in the darkness of her bedroom. As he quietly closed the door behind him, she began to hum.

Candlelight guided him across the hall and back to the bathroom. Georges lay on the floor in a heap, a large portion of his skull missing. In that moment, Olivier felt a myriad of emotions. Grief was not one of them.

He was relieved. He felt a certain since of tranquility at knowing that he would never have to sit through another tense day with his father finding a reason to hurt his mother.

Olivier steadied his breathing – told himself to calm down. There was no one around for miles. All he had to do was get rid of him. He walked down to the parlor and grabbed his father's blanket from the couch. Back upstairs, he rolled Georges in the blanket and drug him down the stairs and out to the yard. Outside the wind cooled his sweat drenched skin. He ran to the garage and grabbed a shovel. He picked a spot just beyond his mother's garden farther downhill of the house and started digging.

He measured the hole, wanting it deep enough that

Georges would not be dug up by wild animals or accidentally

exposed to the elements. He worked for some time with his

thoughts on his mother and what their lives would be like now

that Georges was gone. Once he finished burying his father, he

planned to remove him from the house as well. He would

erase any reminder of him. Soon it would be as though he

never existed.

Olivier threw the shovel aside then pulled Georges over

to the hole where he unceremoniously dumped him inside

before hurriedly covering the hole with dirt. When the grave

was filled, he took a step back to admire his handiwork. For a

finishing touch, he raced to the barn and came back with

chicken wire and a flashlight.

After erecting the makeshift fence, he filled the interior

with trash.

Satisfied with his father's grave, Olivier walked back to

the house and here and there kicked dirt over spots of blood.

Before he entered the back door, he removed his shoes and

clothes. Inside the house, he carefully cleaned the kitchen

floor, removing any droplets of blood that had fallen when he dragged Georges across the floor.

In the bathroom, he cleansed the floor and walls of Georges' blood, working well into the morning until the bathroom gleamed white. Afterward, red tinged water washed from his body and down the drain of the tub.

Exhausted, Olivier went to his room and donned his pajamas. He would stay home from school to be with his mother. He crossed the hall to her bedroom where he climbed into bed beside her. When his head touched the pillow she turned to him – reached out to lay a hand on his cheek.

"Olivier?"

"It's okay, Maman," he reassured her. "I buried him on his feet."

Wardy's eyes burned like pools of flame.

He knew that he had been shoved inside the small shed when the flimsy wooden door slammed closed behind him.

He didn't need to see the dog. He knew it was there.

When the animal attacked, it went straight for his throat.

Toni staggered barefoot along a gravel road. A long

time had passed since he shoved her from the truck. She

could hear water and so she stumbled blindly toward it. The

swamp sat ten feet ahead of her but she could not see. Her

eyes burned like pools of flame.

CHAPTER EIGHT

Five months later...

The first time she saw them together was in town at the brand new strip mall where Delphine's shop sat. She sat across the street in her car in the parking lot of the hardware store. When they left the shop together, Eugene waited on the curb while Delphine locked up and then they strolled arm-in-arm down the sidewalk together for the entire world to see.

Delphine's dark skin glowed with happiness. The dress she wore complemented her curvaceous form and her hair was pulled back with a ribbon. When she turned, Stella clasped her hands to her mouth with surprise at the noticeable bump where Delphine's hands rested on her midriff.

Delphine threw her head back and laughed when Eugene whispered in her ear. He was as strikingly handsome as always – his kinky hair and beard neatly groomed, his broad shoulders and strong back covered in a navy blue button down shirt. She watched their retreating backs with tears in her eyes.

Unable to help herself, Stella started the car and trailed them for blocks before they finally turned down Pruberry Ave., a quiet neighborhood that set in the center of town. She watched as they strode up the walk of a red brick home whose lawn was a lush green. Tulips lined the walk. On the porch, a swing swayed lopsided. She imagined that she could hear Delphine's husky laughter as the two of them disappeared into the house together.

With revenge on her mind, Stella turned and made her way home – fuming, driving too fast with tears of rage streaming down her cheeks.

A week passed before Eugene came home sloppy drunk but in high spirits. He stumbled into the house, giving a deep groan as he fell into his chair to remove his shoes. He ignored Stella when she came to pace the floor in front of him in her night clothes.

"Anything you wanna tell me, Eugene?"

"What you talking about?" he asked after a hearty yawn.

"You son of a bitch," she spat. Her eyes burned with hatred.

Eugene looked up at her with innocent eyes but the expression on her face told him that she knew all she needed to know.

He sighed. "Don't worry, Stella. I'll do right by you."

"Oh, Eugene," Stella cried out in exasperation. She did not know if the pain she felt was from heart break or a bruised ego.

Eugene struggled to his feet, slightly staggering as he rose and playfully reached for her but she backed away and he lost his balance. As he tripped over his own feet and careened toward the floor, their eyes met and held – Eugene in a panic, reaching for Stella with outstretched arms and pleading eyes and Stella staring down at him without remorse, but in spite of her rage she yelled out at the audible *crack* when his head struck the metal corner of a cocktail table.

His eyes were wide open. He was dead before he hit the floor.

EPILOGUE

Olivier stared up at his mother and enjoyed the warmth of her soft, fragrant palms cradling his face, her delicate brown fingers exploring his eyebrows in her special way of seeing him. They stood together in the garden where he'd brought her to stand amongst the flowers. Their sweet aroma caused a soft smile to light her features. The sun was warm on their faces. Even the tail less litter cats that lived in the barn lazed about in the sun.

"How do I look, Olivier?"

Olivier knew why she was asking but he kept his features impassive beneath her prying fingers. His body remained relaxed.

"Your dress is white, Maman, with little red flowers," he said, referring to the long, cotton dress that she wore, strapless but long enough that it fluttered around her ankles. One thick, braided rope of hair fell over her slender shoulder and dark tendrils escaped around her brow. "You are beautiful – like a doll."

"Mon bebe," she cooed. Her fingers hovered over his eyes. "I will always love you."

www.ingramcontent.com/pod-product-compliance
Lightning Source LLC
Chambersburg PA
CBHW022150170626
46807CB00005B/2152